A NIGHTMARE
ON CLOWN STREET

GOOSEBUMPS®
HALL OF HORRORS

#1 CLAWS!
#2 NIGHT OF THE GIANT EVERYTHING
#3 SPECIAL EDITION: THE FIVE MASKS OF DR. SCREEM
#4 WHY I QUIT ZOMBIE SCHOOL
#5 DON'T SCREAM!
#6 THE BIRTHDAY PARTY OF NO RETURN

GOOSEBUMPS® WANTED:
THE HAUNTED MASK

GOOSEBUMPS®
MOST WANTED

#1 PLANET OF THE LAWN GNOMES
#2 SON OF SLAPPY
#3 HOW I MET MY MONSTER
#4 FRANKENSTEIN'S DOG
#5 DR. MANIAC WILL SEE YOU NOW
#6 CREATURE TEACHER: FINAL EXAM
#7 A NIGHTMARE ON CLOWN STREET

SPECIAL EDITION #1 ZOMBIE HALLOWEEN
SPECIAL EDITION #2 THE 12 SCREAMS OF CHRISTMAS
SPECIAL EDITION #3 TRICK OR TRAP

GOOSEBUMPS®
Also available as ebooks

ALSO AVAILABLE:

MOST WANTED

A NIGHTMARE ON CLOWN STREET

R.L. STINE

SCHOLASTIC INC.

ISBN 978-0-545-62774-0

Goosebumps book series created by Parachute Press, Inc.
Copyright © 2015 by Scholastic Inc.

22 21 20 19   19   20/0

Printed in the U.S.A.   40
First printing, March 2015

WELCOME. YOU ARE MOST WANTED.

Come in. I'm R.L. Stine. Welcome to the Goosebumps office.

Have a seat. Yes, I know. It smells a little weird. Ernie, my zombie friend, was here this morning. I asked him, "Why the surprise visit?" Ernie said he was bored. Things were dead at his house.

I asked Ernie what he'd like to do. He said he would *kill* for some lunch. Unfortunately, he *meant* it.

Ernie said he was on a diet. No in-between-meal snacks. Just three servings of human flesh a day.

Well, I see you are admiring the WANTED posters on the wall. Those posters show the creepiest, crawliest, grossest Goosebumps characters of all time. They are the MOST WANTED characters from the MOST WANTED books.

That poster you are studying is of Murder the Clown. Why do they call him *Murder*? Because he *kills* the audience!

Don't pay attention to the axe buried in Murder's head. He is actually a very good clown. He just happens to work at the most frightening circus on earth.

A boy named Ray Gordon can tell you all about it. Ray is about to wish that he'd never visited the circus.

Go ahead. Read Ray's story. You will find out why Murder the Clown is MOST WANTED.

1

I guess it all started when my friend Heather James and I sneaked out of my house and crept down the street to the little circus two blocks away. If I had known what frightening surprises the summer held in store for me, would I have stayed home that night?

I don't think so.

My name is Ray Gordon, and I'm twelve. People call me Ray Gun — even my parents — I guess because I'm kind of explosive. I mean, I don't like to sit still. I'm always shooting off in different directions.

My dad is an artist for an ad agency here in Tampa. Dad can sit at his computer for hours working on one drawing. I can barely sit through a morning of school.

Anyway, Heather came over after dinner to work on our science project. Heather is short and very thin, with a ponytail of light brown hair, pale green eyes, and a lot of freckles. She wore a bright green T-shirt over white shorts.

Our parents are best friends. So Heather and I grew up together like brother and sister. Sometimes we *fight* like brother and sister. She's the careful type. She likes to be the good girl. She thinks I'm a little crazy because I don't always think about what I do.

Like the time I found that miniature horse walking in the empty lot down the street and tried to keep it in my room. But let's not talk about that.

Heather and I sat across from each other at my kitchen table. We had a bowl of nacho chips and a bowl of pretzels in front of us.

I could hear voices down the hall. My parents' book club was meeting in our den.

We couldn't agree on what our science project should be. I said we should do a study on invisibility and bring in an invisible project to school. That would be totally easy.

Heather rolled her eyes. She didn't like that idea.

I said, "We could do some experiments with different liquids. See which ones your dog Clyde will drink."

Heather hit the tabletop with her fist. "No way. I'm not giving Clyde weird things to drink."

"Even for an *A* in science?" I said.

4

"Shut up, Ray," she replied. "I think we should do something with soil."

"Huh? Soil? You mean like *dirt*?"

"We could get different kinds of soil and try to grow stuff in them," Heather said.

"You're kidding, right? Gardening? Why don't you just kill me now?" I groaned.

This was going nowhere. I had a better idea than working on this project. Actually, I'd been planning it all day.

I pushed my chair back and stood up. "Follow me," I said. I waved her toward the kitchen door.

Her green eyes flashed. "Where are we going?" she demanded.

I raised a finger to my lips. "Ssssh."

I could hear a woman reading something out loud in the den. I didn't want my parents to know Heather and I were going out. It's no fun to sneak out if people know about it.

I pulled open the kitchen door. The warm evening air blew in. "We'll have an adventure," I said.

"No. Really," Heather said. "We have to stay and work on this project. We're already late, and we don't have a clue what we're doing."

But I stepped out into the backyard. I knew Heather would follow me.

The air felt hot, as if I'd stepped into an oven. My parents keep the air conditioning cranked up pretty high. The sun had just gone down. The sky was streaked gray and purple. A bird cooed from somewhere in the lemon tree at the back of the yard.

Heather bumped me from behind. "Where are we going, Ray?"

"It's a surprise," I said, moving along the side of the house toward the street.

"And we're doing this *because*?"

I turned back to her and whispered, "Because we're going to join the circus."

2

"We're *what*?" She stopped walking and crossed her arms in front of her. She squinted at me the way she often does, like I'm some kind of nut job.

"A joke," I said. "Just joking. Come on, Heather. We're going to the empty lot. Two blocks, that's all."

"The empty lot?" She trotted to catch up to me. "You found another mini horse?"

"Hey, I told you never to mention that again — remember?"

We both laughed.

We crossed the street. Our neighborhood is usually quiet and empty. But cars jammed the next block. Dozens of people were walking along the curb. They were all heading to the empty lot.

As we came closer, I could see the tall, brown canvas tent. Red and white lights flashed around it. Marching band music floated in the air.

"It's a circus," I told Heather. "A little one-tent circus."

She sniffed. "Mmmmm. I can smell the popcorn."

People were crossing the grassy field, hurrying toward the tent. I heard some kids shouting: "Ray Gun! Hey, Ray Gun!" Kids from our school with their parents. I flashed them a thumbs-up.

We passed the popcorn booth. A sign over the window said CORN POPPED WHILE U WAIT. In the next booth, two women were spinning cones of green-and-purple cotton candy. Ahead of us, a bald man in a white apron carried a tray of salted pretzels.

"Too bad I had a big supper," Heather said.

"We didn't come here for the food," I told her. "We came for the circus show."

She squinted at me. "Since when are you into circuses?"

"Since my uncle Theo visited last year," I said. "He's a clown in another circus. And he's the most awesome guy. He's so funny. You'd love him."

The big red-and-gold sign over the entrance to the tent read: FINGER BROS. CIRCUS. My uncle had told me about the Finger brothers. They had little circuses all over Florida.

"I Googled this circus," I said. "I can't wait to see the white tiger. It's one of the rarest tigers in the world."

She shook her head. "Wow. You really *are* into circuses."

"My uncle Theo got me interested," I said. I heard a trumpeting roar from somewhere behind the big tent. Probably one of the elephants showing off.

The music on the loudspeakers cut off, and a voice announced: "The big show is about to begin. Take your seats, everyone. Take your seats."

I saw two ticket booths at the opening to the show tent. Each booth had a man in a red ringmaster coat and tall top hat taking tickets from the people pouring in.

I started to the opening, but Heather grabbed my arm and pulled me back.

"Hey, let go. The show is starting," I said.

"Ray, I didn't bring any money," she said. "Do you have any for the tickets?"

I shook my head.

"Then how are we going to get in?" she asked.

"No worries," I said. "We'll sneak in."

3

"No way!" Heather cried. She grabbed my arm and pulled me across the grass. "Come on. We're going back to your house to think up a science project."

I tugged my arm free. "We're going to sneak in. It's easy," I told her. "We'll just walk right in."

"You're crazy, Ray. You really are nutsoid."

"Heather, don't you like adventure?" I said.

"No," she replied. "Actually, I *hate* adventure. Especially when it means we're going to be caught. And arrested. And if we're not arrested, we'll be totally embarrassed. And I *hate* to be embarrassed."

"I really want to see the white tiger," I said. "This is our chance. Follow me and don't act guilty."

"Excuse me?" she cried. "Don't act guilty? What does *that* mean?"

I pointed. "See how big groups of people are walking in? They're in a hurry because the show is starting. So, we just wait for a bunch of people to walk in together. And we get into the middle of them and go in with them."

I took her hand and started to lead her to the tent. "I'm not happy about this," she said. "Seriously. I'm not happy."

"Stop being so tense," I said. "We're practically in."

I waited by the side of the tent entrance till a group of seven or eight people approached a ticket booth. "Come on," I said. "This is it."

Heather and I pushed past two or three of them and worked our way into the middle of their group. We all started walking into the tent.

"Hey, you kids!"

I jumped and a startled squeak escaped my throat. A stern voice boomed: "Stop right there. Where do you think *you're* going? I'm calling the police."

Okay. So Plan A didn't work.

The two ticket-takers in top hats blocked our path. "Sorry, kids. No pay, no play," the taller one said.

"I ... uh ... left my tickets at home," I said.

"Well, why don't you run home and get them," he said. "We'll wait for you right here."

Heather dug an elbow into my ribs. She had her teeth clamped together and she was growling like a tiger about to attack. I figured she wasn't too happy with me.

I turned away from the ticket-takers and began walking along the side of the tent.

Heather followed, still growling. Her hands were balled into tight fists. "Okay. Now everyone knows we're pitiful losers. Can we go back to your house?" she asked through clenched teeth.

"A quitter never wins," I said.

"And what does that mean?"

"It means I have another idea," I said. I tripped over one of the big spikes that the tent ropes were wrapped around. I stumbled and fell onto my stomach on the grass.

Heather laughed.

"You have a great sense of humor," I said. I picked myself up. "Now, here's my plan. . . ."

Heather crossed her arms in front of her. "How much do I want to hear this?" she asked.

I ignored her sarcasm. "I saw this old movie," I told her. "These kids wanted to see the circus. So they sneaked in through the back of the show tent."

Heather growled at me again.

"Did you have your rabies shot?" I said.

That made her laugh. She shook her head, her light brown ponytail waving behind her. "You're impossible, Ray."

"Check it out. There's no one at the back of the tent," I told her. "We lift the canvas and crawl inside. No problem."

"The only problem is with your *brain*," she muttered. But she followed me around the side of the tent.

It suddenly grew very dark. All the lights were in the front. The voices of all the people faded into the distance. I could hear crickets chirping.

I turned to Heather. "See? We're all alone back here."

She glanced around. "It's kind of creepy."

I ran my hand along the tent canvas. "I don't see any flap or anything," I said. "But I still think we can slip under the canvas."

I leaned over and gripped the tent bottom with both hands. The canvas was heavy and tied down tightly. This wasn't going to be easy. But I tugged with all my strength and got it about a foot off the ground.

"Go ahead. Crawl in," I said to Heather.

That's when I saw the giant.

I gasped as a huge man stepped out of the shadows. He was at least seven feet tall and as wide as a truck. His face was hidden in darkness. But even in the dim light, I could see the powerful muscles on his arms, his enormous hands balled into fists.

I was still holding the tent canvas as he stomped up to Heather and me.

"Hey," he boomed. He had a voice like thunder. "Caught you! Do you know what we do to people who try to sneak in? *Do* you?"

"N-no," I stammered. "What do you do?"

"We don't do *anything*!" the giant man boomed. Then he roared with laughter.

I dropped the canvas. I stepped back. Heather's eyes were wide with fright. She bumped into me as we both backed away from the tent.

As the big man came closer, I could see the white clown makeup on his face. He had a bald head, a wide painted smile that went nearly from ear to ear. And big tufts of fluffy hair that poked up from his ears.

"Did I scare you?" he asked, his voice soft now. His dark eyes moved from Heather to me.

"A little," I confessed.

He thumped the chest of his clown shirt with a thumb. "I'm Tiny," he said. "That's my name. Tiny. Have you seen the circus?"

"No," I answered. "We wanted to, but we didn't have any money."

"It was all Ray's idea," Heather said. "I don't want to be a snitch. But if you want to turn someone in to security or something, it was all his idea."

I rolled my eyes. "Thanks a bunch, Heather."

"I'm glad you like the circus so much," Tiny said. "I was looking for my partner. I work with a dwarf clown named Biggie. We're Biggie and Tiny."

My heart stopped pounding like a drum in my chest. I started to relax. Tiny was friendly. Not menacing at all.

A warm breeze fluttered the tent. Heather swept her hair back with one hand. I could see she wasn't worried anymore. And she had stopped growling at me.

"Once, we caught a guy sneaking in," Tiny said. "He loved the circus so much, we put him to work."

"Awesome," I murmured.

Tiny scratched one ear. "Well, we told him he could clean the animal cages. He got all excited. He couldn't believe he was actually working at the circus."

Tiny leaned closer. "Only there was a slight problem," he said. "We forgot to tell the guy one thing. We forgot to tell him he wasn't supposed to clean the tiger cage with the tiger still in it."

Heather gasped.

Tiny burst out laughing. "Hahahaha! What a mess that was. It took four of us to clean *him* up." He laughed some more.

"You're joking — right?" Heather said.

He nodded. "Maybe." It was hard to see his expression beneath the white clown makeup and the huge, painted grin.

"My uncle Theo is a clown, too," I said.

Tiny turned to me. "Where does he work?"

"He works for a traveling circus," I said. "It's called Koko's Klown Academy."

"I've heard of it," Tiny said. He scratched the big tuft of hair on his ear again. "It's an all-clown circus, right?"

"I think so," I said. "I've never seen it. My uncle keeps promising to let me work at his circus one summer, but —"

"Well, don't clean the tiger cage!" Tiny said, and he bellowed with laughter again.

"Uncle Theo loves being a clown," I said when he finally stopped.

"Yeah. Me too, kid. Being a clown is a good life. As long as you stay away from Clown Street, you're golden."

I blinked. "Huh? Clown Street? What's that?"

Tiny opened his mouth to answer. But a loud shout interrupted. "Hey! There you are!"

I spun around to see my dad running toward us over the grass. He was waving one hand at us wildly.

"Uh-oh," I muttered.

17

Dad came tearing up to the tent, breathing hard. He's not much of an athlete. He sits in front of a computer all day.

He nodded to Tiny. Then he turned angrily to Heather and me. "What are you doing here? I've been looking for you for nearly an hour."

"S-sorry," I stammered.

Dad grabbed my elbow and started to lead me away. "You two are supposed to be doing homework, right?"

"It was all Ray's idea," Heather said, trotting to keep up with Dad and me.

"Of course it was," Dad said. "You didn't need to tell me that."

I turned back. Tiny still stood at the back of the show tent. "Tiny," I yelled. "What's Clown Street?"

He cupped his hands around his mouth and shouted, "You don't want to know!"

Dad drove Heather home. He didn't talk much in the car. He just kept shaking his head and muttering under his breath.

Mom was in the kitchen. She sat at the table, going through a pile of bills. "Where was he?" she asked Dad without looking up.

Dad sighed. He pulled a bottle of water from the fridge. "At the circus down the street," he said.

"Ray, were you planning to join the circus?" Mom asked.

"Ha-ha. Funny," I muttered.

She finally turned to me. Mom is very pretty. She has straight blond hair, round blue eyes, and a terrific smile. She used to model for the ad agency Dad works for here in Tampa.

My friends are always telling me how I have the hottest mom in town. It's kind of a weird thing to hear all the time.

19

She frowned at me. "Ray Gun, I'm upset with you."

I lowered my head. "Sorry. You see, Heather and I couldn't decide on a science project. So I thought maybe the circus would give us some fresh ideas."

Was she buying it? No.

"Fresh ideas at the circus? Seriously?" She shook her head. "You'll have to do better than that, Ray."

Dad set down his water bottle. "Just another one of your crazy ideas, huh, buddy?"

Mom picked up an envelope and waved it at me. "We have an invitation for you. But now we don't know if you can be trusted."

"An invitation? What is it?" I made a grab for the envelope, but Mom swiped it out of my reach.

"It's from your uncle Theo," Mom said.

I felt a burst of excitement. "And he wants me to come stay with him at the circus all summer?" I cried.

Mom glanced at Dad. Then she nodded. "Your dad and I aren't sure you're ready to go off on your own like that. Especially after you pull a stunt like sneaking out of the house tonight."

"Of *course* I'm ready!" I cried. "I'm twelve years old. I'm not a kid."

"But you do crazy things," Dad said. "You're too impulsive. You —"

"Is that a yes?" I cried. "Uncle Theo will look out for me. You know he's a good guy. We talked about this when he visited. He said I could work with him and he'd take care of me."

"Well . . ." Mom hesitated, waving the envelope in her hand.

"Can I go? Please? Can I go?"

"Okay," they both said at once.

I jumped into the air, screaming. Only two weeks till school was out. I knew this was going to be the most exciting summer of my life.

Two weeks later, Koko's Klown Academy was playing in Jacksonville. So it wasn't a very long bus ride for me.

My parents packed up nearly everything I owned into two big suitcases. They took me to the bus station. And they both gave me about a thousand warnings not to be crazy and to follow every word my uncle said.

I promised and promised. I raised my right hand and swore to be perfect.

I'm not sure they believed me.

As the bus made its way north to Jacksonville, I wanted to think about Uncle Theo's circus and what kind of job he had in mind for me. But the teenager in the seat next to me stayed on his phone arguing with his girlfriend for the whole trip. I couldn't think about anything.

I was so happy when the bus pulled into the

Jacksonville station. I jumped down and waited for the driver to pull out my two bags. It was a hot, humid day. The sun kept peeking out from high clouds. There was no breeze at all.

I pulled my suitcases to the curb. Then I shielded my eyes with one hand and searched for Uncle Theo.

No sign of him.

Was he waiting for me inside the station?

Before I could pick up my suitcases, I saw someone moving fast across the parking lot.

Whoa!

A terrifying-looking, red-faced man *with an axe buried in his head*!

He came charging at me like a stampeding bull, waving both arms, shrieking in panic: "Murder! Murder!"

7

I laughed. "Uncle Theo, you look different," I said.

"Ray, that's because you've never seen me with an axe in my head."

He wrapped me in a hug. "Good to see you. I'm so happy you're here."

I stepped back and studied him. Theo's clown name is Murder the Clown. Even though he was dressed in a ragged, long, polka-dot jacket and baggy yellow pants, he looked totally evil.

His face was painted bright red. His mouth was hidden inside a thick, black scowl. His painted black eyebrows stretched down the sides of his face. His curly golden wig was split down the middle by the blood-spattered hatchet that appeared to be buried deep in the top of his head.

Instead of a clown ruffle, he had a fat brown snake around his neck. It was fake, of course, but very real looking. Its jaws were open wide, its fangs ready to bite.

"Uncle Theo, do you always walk around town in your clown makeup?" I asked.

"The circus makes us stay in costume whenever we're out in public," he said. He picked up my suitcases. I followed him into the bus station.

A small crowd had gathered to stare at him. He set down the bags and walked over to them. I saw his eyes flash with excitement. Last year when he visited, he told me how much he loved to entertain an audience.

He leaned close to a man in work overalls who had two little redheaded boys at his sides. "Have you seen an axe anywhere?" he asked. "I know I had one, but I can't find it."

The man gazed at the axe in Murder's head and smiled. But the two little boys backed away. I could see they were frightened.

"I'd lose my head if it wasn't glued on!" Murder said. He turned to the little boys. "Don't be scared of *me*," he barked at them. "Have you looked in the mirror lately? You could scare *yourself*!"

Some people in the small crowd laughed.

But the father shook his head angrily. "You shouldn't scare little boys," he told Murder.

"Why should *parents* have all the fun?" Murder exclaimed. He tossed back his head and let out a long, evil laugh.

"Ooh, I have such a headache!" Murder cried, pointing to the axe in his head. "Such a headache! You might call it a *splitting* headache!

Hahaha! Do you know what I have a sudden craving for? *Chop* suey! Hahahaha!"

A little boy in red shorts and a *Power Rangers* T-shirt stepped up to Murder. "I saw you in the circus," he said.

"I saw you there, too," Murder told him. "In the monkey cage. You were showing off your pink butt! Hahahaha!"

A large woman in a green sundress and a Tampa Bay Rays cap frowned at Murder. "You're not funny. You're making the kids cry."

"Your *face* is making *me* cry!" Murder shouted. "Hahaha. It's Murder! MURDER!"

The crowd liked that. Most people laughed. The two little redheaded boys still hid behind their father.

"Know why they call me Murder the Clown?" he boomed. "Because I *kill*! My jokes *kill* the audience! I murder them! Hahahaha!"

He pulled off his fake nose and gave it to one of the redheaded boys. "Know why I gave you that nose? Because you *smell*! Hahaha!"

I laughed along with the other people. I couldn't help but laugh. Murder was so mean, he was funny. A few people were upset by his humor. But most of the crowd was still laughing as he picked up my bags and we walked across the parking lot.

He led the way to a red-white-and-blue circus van. He tossed my suitcases in the back and then turned to me. "It's all in good fun, kid," he said. "You've got to keep it fun. You don't want to end up on Clown Street."

I tugged at his baggy sleeve. "Uncle Theo, tell me," I said. "What is Clown Street?"

"Well —"

Before he could answer, the father and the two redheaded boys stepped up to us. The father shrugged and motioned to his sons. "They've decided they want your autograph," he told my uncle.

"Good kids," Murder said. He reached into the van and pulled out a pen that was three feet long. "Why do I need this pen? Because I have a *very long* name!" he said.

The boys laughed.

Murder pulled out photos of himself and signed them. Then we drove from the bus station to the circus grounds, which were only a few blocks away. He pulled the van into a parking lot at the back. "Let's take a walk," he said. "Give you a chance to see where everything is."

The afternoon sun was high in the sky. The back of my neck prickled from the heat as we walked across a grassy square. I wished I had remembered my sunglasses.

I could see the tall red-and-blue show tent in the distance. In front of us, I saw two long rows of carnival booths. We passed a kiddie merry-go-round and roller coaster.

The rides were full, and crowds of people, mostly in shorts and T-shirts, jammed the carnival area. "The afternoon show doesn't start till four," Uncle Theo said. "But people come early for the carnival games and the food."

I suddenly realized I hadn't eaten since breakfast back home. I pulled Murder to a food booth called *Katz's Dogs.* "Two wiener dogs with everything on them," Murder told the young woman behind the counter. He whispered to me, "They use real dogs. Nothing artificial."

After we gobbled our hot dogs, we walked through the carnival area. People waved and pointed at Murder. Some joker shouted, "Do you know you have an axe in your head?"

Murder slapped his forehead like he was surprised. "No *wonder* I'm seeing double! Know what I need right now? A banana *split*! Hahaha!"

We continued walking. He whispered to me, "Murder. I *murder* them!"

At the booth across from us, kids were tossing darts at a wall of balloons. In the next booth, people threw large plastic rings at fish bowls, trying to win goldfish. A wheel-of-fortune booth had huge pink teddy bears as a prize.

A wide food trailer had a sign on its side: ALL-YOU-CAN-EAT ON A STICK! I took a deep breath and inhaled the aroma of French fries from inside. Nice.

"I think I'm going to like it here!" I told my uncle.

Before he could answer, a polka-dot-costumed clown on stilts clomped up to us. "Hey, Short Stuff," he called down to Murder. "You'd better get out of the sun. Your face is bright red!"

"You'd better come down from there," Murder told him. "*Your* face is scaring the birds!" Murder put a hand on my shoulder. "This is my nephew Ray." He pointed up to the other clown. "His name is Mr. Funny. Know why we call him that?"

"Because he's funny?" I said.

Murder shook his head. "No. Because that's his name! Hahahaha!"

Mr. Funny wobbled on his stilts. "Your uncle is about as funny as an ingrown toenail. No. I'm wrong. He's about as funny as *five* ingrown toenails! Welcome to the circus, kid." He staggered off on the stilts, waving his hands above his head.

We started to walk again. "I'll introduce you to the other clowns later," my uncle said. "We all meet in the food tent an hour before the afternoon show and have snacks and stuff."

Two teenage girls racing with cones of cotton candy almost knocked us over. Giggling, they kept running. Murder adjusted the axe on his head. "This thing is heavy," he complained. "People don't realize how uncomfortable it is to have an axe in your head." He grinned. "But . . . that's show biz."

We passed another Lucky Wheel booth and a shooting gallery. Across from them, I saw a large glass tank filled with water. A clown was perched on a seat high above the water tank. A sign on the front of the tank read: DUNK-A-KLOWN.

I started toward it. But to my surprise, Uncle Theo grabbed me by the shoulders and spun me around. "Keep walking. Just ignore that," he said. He suddenly sounded tense.

I tried to turn back to the tank, but he held me in place. "It looks cool," I said.

"Stay away from it, Ray. I'm being serious. Let's just keep walking, okay?"

What was his problem?

We started past the tank. I glimpsed the clown again, sitting stiffly on the metal seat. He wore a blond wig that stood straight up over a pale, sad face.

In front of the tank, a teenage boy was tossing baseballs at a target. As I watched, one of his throws hit the target. A loud buzzer went off. The clown's chair collapsed.

The clown raised his hands high above his head as he dropped into the deep water tank. The crowd cheered.

30

The clown splashed into the water, sending a tall wave against the glass. I watched him sink to the bottom of the tank. His hands thrashed the water. He struggled to pull himself to the top.

"Keep walking," Uncle Theo said. "Don't look at that."

But I heard a loud flushing sound. Like a huge toilet flushing. And I saw the water in the tank start to sink. The clown thrashed the water with his hands and feet as he was sucked down . . . down . . . In seconds, the water had drained. The clown had vanished with it. The last thing I saw was his tall blond wig. Then it vanished, too.

The crowd cheered again. Some people laughed. They thought it was funny. But I wasn't so sure.

"Uncle Theo," I said. "Where did that clown go? Why did he look so frightened?"

Uncle Theo laughed. "It's all a gag, Ray. Everything is a joke here. Remember? This is an all-clown circus. You can't believe what you see. Nothing is real."

Nothing is real?

I stared at the empty water tank. If that wasn't real, why did the clown struggle so much? And why did he look totally terrified?

At three o'clock, people were lined up, waiting for the show tent to open. Uncle Theo led me to a smaller tent around the back.

We had to step around a young woman in a sparkly gold costume who was brushing the back of an elephant with a big shoe brush. The elephant stood perfectly still. But its eyes followed Uncle Theo and me as we passed.

A bunch of clowns were waiting to greet me outside the food tent. I guessed Uncle Theo had told them about me. They cheered as we came near.

"A new victim!" one of them yelled.

"Kid — you're *history*! You're dead meat! Hahaha!"

"Welcome to Koko's Klown Academy! You already flunked! Ha-ha!"

They cheered and laughed at their own jokes.

"Give the kid a break," Uncle Theo said. "It's murder! Murder! You're killing the kid!"

They didn't wait for him to introduce me. Two clowns rushed forward and lifted me off my feet. "Hey — put me down!" I cried. "Where are we going?"

All the clowns followed, laughing and clapping, as the two clowns carried me on their shoulders around the side of a tent. I saw the trampoline in front of us. They heaved me onto it.

A very fat clown with a white face, tall pointed hat, and red ruffles over his white clown suit climbed onto the trampoline with me. He began to jump.

I was bounced hard. I flew into the air. I toppled down, then flew up again.

"Go, kid, go!"

"Are you feeling jumpy?"

The clowns whooped and cheered as I jumped and bounced along with the big clown. "Hey!" I shouted as the fat clown bounced harder. I couldn't keep my balance. I flew off the trampoline. As I headed for the ground, two clowns caught me and eased me to the grass.

I struggled to catch my breath.

The fat clown climbed down. He stood beside me. "How did you like it?"

"I loved it!" I said. "Can we go again?"

They all burst out laughing at my answer. They clapped me so hard on the back, I nearly fell over.

"That's our welcoming ceremony," Uncle Theo said. "What do you expect from a bunch of clowns?"

He introduced me to them. A sad, bald clown dressed as a bum in a ragged brown suit, with tears painted on his cheeks over a thick stubble of beard, was named Tommy Teardrops. The fat clown who bounced with me on the trampoline was Billy Laffs. A woman clown with big red makeup circles on her cheeks, a red Raggedy Ann wig, big red shoes, and a huge butt that had to be two pillows under her long dress, introduced herself as Mrs. Giggle-Wiggle.

I met at least a dozen clowns. Uncle Theo said, "Don't worry. You'll have plenty of time to learn their names. Let's eat."

We all went into the tent. I saw two rows of long picnic tables and a food table against the far tent wall. I lined up with the others and helped myself to a turkey sandwich and a pile of nacho chips.

A tall clown with a bird's nest of curly black hair bouncing on his head balanced a banana on his nose. "Hey, has anyone seen my banana?" he shouted.

"Ray, do you know why he has that banana on his nose?" Billy Laffs asked me.

"No," I said.

"I don't, either!" Billy replied.

That got a pretty good laugh from everyone.

"At least I'm well-balanced," the tall clown said. "At least I have a-peel!"

The clowns sat down at the long tables to have their snack. I sat next to Uncle Theo, who had piled his plate high with cookies and pretzels. "My two favorite food groups," he said.

The clowns joked and teased one another as they ate. Two clowns at different tables tossed apples back and forth. They started with two apples, but kept adding more until there were five apples flying back and forth in the air.

Then, suddenly, a hush fell over the tent.

The apples stopped flying. The clowns went silent.

I turned to the tent entrance and saw a new clown enter. He wore the red jacket and black top hat of a ringmaster. He was a big man, broad-shouldered, like a body builder.

His face was painted white. He had black circles around his eyes, a thin mustache under his red clown nose. His mouth was covered in black makeup, twisted into a sneer.

Uncle Theo bumped me with his elbow. "Shhh," he whispered. "It's the boss."

I glanced down the table. The other clowns had their eyes down. No one spoke.

Are they all afraid of him? I wondered.

Uncle Theo jumped to his feet. "Mr. HahaFace, I'd like you to meet my nephew," he said.

The ringmaster's black boots thudded the ground as he strode across the tent to us. He kept his eyes on me as he walked.

"Remember? I told you my nephew was arriving for the summer?" Uncle Theo said. "Well, here he is. He's going to be a junior clown."

Mr. HahaFace studied me for a long moment. *Talk about an awkward silence.*

Finally, the ringmaster stuck his hand out for me to shake. "I hope you're funny, Jack," he said.

"But my name is Ray," I said.

Some clowns raised their fingers to their lips. They were telling me to be quiet.

I felt a chill at the back of my neck. Why were they all so frightened of the ringmaster?

"Welcome to our little world, Jack," Mr. HahaFace said. "I'm sure you will make your uncle proud. And I'm sure you'll learn a lot this summer."

"I — I'll try," I stammered.

Then Mr. HahaFace reached under his red jacket and pulled out a huge needle. A doctor's needle for giving shots, only it was more than a foot long!

"Someone hold Jack in place," he ordered.

Uncle Theo didn't move. But two other clowns stepped up behind me and grabbed my shoulders.

"Give me your arm, Jack," the ringmaster said. "I need to take a blood sample."

"A blood sample?" I asked. My voice came out high and shaky.

He waved the enormous needle in front of me. "I need to see if you have any clown blood in your veins."

"No. Wait," I said. I swung my arm away from him. "You can't —"

"Hold him still!" Mr. HahaFace shouted. "Don't let him run."

The two clowns gripped my shoulders and held me in place. I shut my eyes as Mr. HahaFace lowered the huge needle to my arm.

10

Silence. I waited for the sharp stab of pain. Gritted my teeth and waited.

I opened my eyes. Mr. HahaFace stood with the big needle in the air. He tossed back his head and laughed.

The other clowns began to laugh, too. But I could tell they were only pretending to laugh.

Mr. HahaFace patted my shoulder. "Relax, Jack. That's a joke I play on all the new people." He chuckled. "Go ahead. Sit down. Enjoy your snack."

He nodded to Uncle Theo, tipped his top hat to the other clowns, and strode out of the tent.

Several clowns let out sighs of relief. I heard low mutters and tense laughter.

I've never been afraid of clowns. But something about Mr. HahaFace totally terrified me.

I turned to my uncle, who had taken his seat beside me. "He's kind of scary," I whispered.

"Kind of," Uncle Theo agreed. He stuffed a cookie into his mouth.

"Why is everyone so afraid of him?" I asked.

Uncle Theo chewed for a long while and swallowed his cookie. He kept his eyes on his food plate. "Just keep clear of him, Ray. Keep clear of him, and you'll have no worries."

"Hey, kid," Billy Laffs called from down the table. "Don't worry about HahaFace. We're all one big happy family here."

"Yeah, if you belonged to a family of SHARKS!" Uncle Theo barked in his Murder the Clown voice. He gave me a playful shove. "Clown life is murder! *Murder!*"

Mrs. Giggle-Wiggle stood up. "The only thing better than being a clown," she shouted, "is being ME!" She wiggled her big pillow butt.

Everyone laughed.

"Speak for yourself!" Billy Laffs said. "I'd rather *see* you than *be* you!"

"I'd rather be a clown than be the circus elephant," another clown cried. "He works for peanuts!"

"Do you know what the monkeys work for?"

"No. What?"

"Same salary as you!"

As the clowns laughed and joked, I turned and glanced around at the other tables. I looked for the yellow-wigged clown from the Dunk-A-Klown

39

tank. I went from face to face. But he wasn't in the tent.

I elbowed Uncle Theo. "Where is the clown from the Dunk-A-Klown tank?" I asked.

He stared at me for a long moment. "I don't know," he said finally. Then he stared down at his plate. He didn't look me in the eye.

I pictured that clown being flushed from the tank, sinking out of sight with that terrified look on his face. And I thought about Mr. HahaFace, how the clowns all grew silent as soon as he entered the room.

Something strange is going on here, I thought. *Something strange and frightening. Something Uncle Theo doesn't want to tell me about.*

11

At the back of the lot, several long trailers and mobile homes were parked in rows. This is where the circus people lived.

Uncle Theo's mobile home was painted bright red and had a painting of his face, axe and all, beside the front door. I climbed the metal steps and followed him inside.

He had a small, yellow-tiled kitchen, a living room with a big leather armchair and a flat screen TV, and a tiny bedroom and bathroom at the other end. The walls were covered with portraits of other clowns, dozens of grinning, painted faces.

He smiled at me. "Pretty nice place, huh?"

"It looks very comfy," I said.

"Yeah, it's cozy." He motioned me into the living room. "I'll take you to your trailer, Ray. As soon as we get you in costume." He disappeared into the bedroom in back.

I dropped onto the small couch across

from the armchair. "I have my own trailer?" I called.

"Well, no. You have to share it," he said. "I think you'll like your roommate. He's a good guy."

He stepped back into the living room carrying a blue-and-white ruffled clown suit and a big pillow. "Try this on." He tossed it to me. "The pillow goes on your stomach."

I laughed. "This is really for *me*?"

He nodded. "For the rest of the summer, your name is Mr. Belly-Bounce."

"Mr. Belly-Bounce." I repeated the name. I didn't really believe it.

"That's your whole act," Uncle Theo said. "You bounce your belly. You practice it till you've got it. Till you're funny." He slapped my shoulder. "You'll kill! You'll *murder* them!"

I laughed and rolled the pillow between my hands. "Well . . . we'll see if I have any clown blood in my veins."

Uncle Theo tugged me to my feet. "Come on. I'll take you to your trailer and you can try on the costume."

He led the way out of his mobile home. I had the pillow in one hand and the clown costume draped over my other arm.

Down the row of trailers, I saw a bald, grinning clown juggling duckpins. He kept dropping them and muttering to himself. Loud hip-hop music poured from another trailer. A clown was busy washing down the front of another mobile home with a hose and a big sponge.

Uncle Theo led me behind the tall show tent. "Your trailer is on the other side," he said, pointing.

We were walking at the back of the show tent when I heard an alarmed shout: "Hey — look out!"

I turned — and screamed — as a knife with a long blade came flying at my head.

No time to duck. I shut my eyes and waited for the crushing pain.

12

I felt the air off the blade as it zinged by my face. Still frozen in place, I opened my eyes. The knife made a ripping sound as it stuck into the tent canvas.

I opened my mouth, but I was too startled to speak.

"Hey — who threw that?" Uncle Theo screamed. He jumped forward, his eyes darting all around the circus lot. "Who threw that?"

My whole body was tingling. It happened so fast, I didn't really have time to be frightened. I stared at the knife handle poking out from the tent canvas. And again, I pictured the long, shiny blade soaring right at my face.

"Who threw that knife?" Uncle Theo screamed.

There was no one in sight.

He turned to me. "Someone thinks I need *another* hole in my head!" he exclaimed. "I told you, it's *murder* around here!"

"It's not funny," I said, finally finding my

voice. "Are you sure that knife was aimed at *you*?"

"Maybe it was an accident," he replied. "I think the knife just slipped away from someone. I don't think they were aiming. And why would someone throw a knife at *you*? No one *knows* you."

My uncle was a bad liar. Even under his thick red face makeup, I could see he wasn't telling the truth. He knew it wasn't an accident.

The sun was going down. Long shadows stretched across the grass. I squinted into the gray light. Beyond the tent, a clown was watering an elephant. Across from him, a clown pushed another clown in a wheelbarrow.

I shuddered. I kept hearing the *zing* of the knife as it whirled past my head.

I still felt shaky as Uncle Theo led the way to a clump of metal trailers at the far end of the lot. They weren't lined up. They were parked at funny angles, as if they'd been tossed there.

The grass gave way to gravel as we stepped up to a trailer. It had a hand-written sign over the door that read: *Top Cat.*

"They all have names so you can find yours easily," my uncle said.

Out in front of the trailer, a clown stood at the side of a ping-pong table. He had a paddle in each hand and appeared to be playing a ping-pong game all by himself.

He stopped slapping the ball and looked up as Uncle Theo and I stepped over to him. He had a painted white face with a red smile from ear to ear. A red light bulb nose twitched beneath big, black eyes. A red yarn wig rested at an angle on his head.

"This is your roommate, Bingo-Bongo," Uncle Theo said. "I've got to run. You guys get to know each other."

He turned and trotted off, his big clown shoes kicking up gravel.

I stepped up to the ping-pong table. "I'm Ray," I said.

"No, you're not," my roommate replied.

"Excuse me?"

"We don't use our real names here," he explained. "Only our clown names."

"I get it," I said. "Well . . . I guess I'm Mr. Belly-Bounce." I held up my costume and the pillow.

He laughed. "Maybe I'll call you Ray."

He bounced the ping-pong ball on the table and began hitting it back and forth over the net. "Bingo-Bongo, Bingo-Bongo," he chanted. "See? My name goes with my act. I play ping-pong by myself." He played faster and faster till I could barely see the ball.

Finally, his left-hand paddle smashed the ball hard. His right hand swiped and missed. "Game over," he said, raising his dark eyes to me. He set the paddles down on the table. I could see sweat forming on his white face makeup.

"That's awesome!" I said. "Is that your whole act?"

"No. Then I do it blindfolded," he replied. "It takes a lot of practice. What's your act?"

"Well ... I guess my act is ... I bounce my belly up and down."

We both laughed.

"That takes skill, too," he said. "You'll see."

A few trailers down, I heard a man and woman arguing loudly. Country music floated out of a trailer behind ours. Next to us, a clown had set up a hammock and was slowly rocking on his back, sound asleep.

"So do I call you Bingo-Bongo?" I asked.

He nodded. "I told you, we don't use our real names here — especially around Mr. HahaFace."

"Tell me," I said. "Why is everyone so afraid of HahaFace?"

"Yes. Tell him," a voice boomed behind me.

I spun around and saw that Mr. HahaFace was standing right there. Had he been eavesdropping?

"Go ahead, Bingo-Bongo," he said. "Why don't you tell him why everyone is afraid of me!"

Bingo-Bongo stumbled and knocked the ping-pong paddles off the table. His eyes went wide with fright.

I stepped back, adjusting the pillow and costume in my arms.

"Well..." Bingo-Bongo said. "I was just explaining some of the rules to Mr. Belly-Bounce, sir. I want to help him rehearse. And I'll help him in the ring tomorrow."

Mr. HahaFace frowned. "And why is everyone scared of me?"

"Uh..." Bingo-Bongo hesitated. "I was about to tell him that *no one* is scared of you. Everyone *respects* you, sir. That's all I was going to say."

Mr. HahaFace studied Bingo-Bongo for a long while. Then he turned his eyes on me. Finally, he said, "Be funny, guys." He tipped his top hat to us, turned, and strode away.

I watched him till he disappeared around the

side of the show tent. "So tell me," I said, "why are you so scared of him?"

Bingo-Bongo shrugged. "He's the boss. That's all." He scowled at me. "I really don't want to talk about it."

"No problem," I said. "Do you think I'll be ready to perform tomorrow?"

"It's easy," he replied. "Bounce your big belly up and down and bump into people. Knock people over with it. That's always funny." He squinted at me. "You're not afraid, are you?"

"No," I answered. "I like adventures. Seriously. I'm *already* the class clown at school!"

He laughed. "Go inside and put on your costume. I'll show you a few things."

A hip-hop beat suddenly burst from our trailer. "Oh. That's my ringtone," Bingo-Bongo said. "I left my phone in there." He scrambled up the steps and disappeared into the trailer.

I gazed around. I suddenly felt happy and excited. Here I was in a new world. It really was like being on a different planet. A clown planet where everyone wore crazy makeup and costumes, and everyone had a funny name.

It was maybe the only place on earth where the only thing everyone cared about was making people laugh.

Could I be a funny clown? Of course. Back home, Heather was always calling me a clown. She didn't know I'd really become one.

I turned and started to follow Bingo-Bongo into the trailer. But I stopped when I saw the door to the trailer next to ours swing open.

A girl clown stepped out. She wore a short, pleated yellow skirt over white tights and a sparkly blue vest. Her blond hair fell around her painted white face. Even with the makeup, I could tell she was about my age.

I walked over to her to introduce myself.

But she spoke first. "I know who you are," she said. "You're the next victim."

14

I gasped. I couldn't hide my shock.

She laughed. "Joking," she said. "See? We're clowns. We're supposed to make jokes."

I could feel myself blushing. "I'm new here," I said. "I just arrived today and —"

"I know," she said. "I'm Deanna Banana. And you're Mr. Belly-Bounce."

"You seem to know everything," I said.

She nodded. "I get around."

"I just got here from Tampa. That's where I live," I said. "Where are you from?"

"Mars."

I laughed. "You don't look like a Martian."

"How do *you* know? Actually, I'm a circus kid. I've lived at this circus my whole life."

"Weird," I said. "What kind of act do you do?"

"I do a knife-throwing act." She pulled a long-bladed knife out from under her vest. She flipped it into the air and caught it on the third spin.

"Hey," I said, "did one of your knives get away from you a few minutes ago?"

She squinted at me. She had round blue eyes. "No. I've been inside." She pointed to her trailer. "But you know what? One of my knives is missing. I counted them this morning, and I couldn't find one."

"Well, someone threw a knife at me," I told her. "Back of the big tent. It just missed my head."

Her painted red mouth formed an O. "Seriously? Why?"

"I don't know," I said. I lowered my voice. "Something funny is going on at this circus, Deanna."

"It's supposed to," she said.

"No. Funny *weird*," I said. "I just got here, but I can tell something is wrong. I mean, my uncle won't answer my questions about Clown Street or the Dunk-A-Klown booth."

She tossed back her long hair. "Really? Do you think he's hiding something?"

I nodded. "Yes. I think something scary is going on. And what's up with that ringmaster?"

"You mean Mr. HahaFace?" she said.

"Yes. He's some kind of freak. Why is everyone so afraid of him? When HahaFace showed up in the food tent, everyone instantly went silent. It was totally weird."

"Yeah. Weird," she repeated.

52

I started to say more. But I was interrupted by a shout from Bingo-Bongo from inside the trailer. "Hey, Belly-Bounce. Where are you?"

"I'd better go inside," I said. "Catch you later."

I turned and hurried into the trailer. It wasn't as luxurious as Uncle Theo's mobile home. I saw two narrow cots, a tiny stove and refrigerator, a counter with two stools for eating, and two folding chairs.

I dropped my costume and the pillow onto the cot against the wall. Then I turned to Bingo-Bongo. He was sprawled on the floor, his back against the trailer wall.

He looked up from his phone. "Who were you talking to out there?"

"The girl from the next trailer," I said.

He lowered his phone. "Deanna Banana?"

I nodded. "Yeah."

He sat up straight. He narrowed his eyes at me. "What did you talk about? You didn't say anything bad about the circus — did you?"

"Well . . ." I hesitated. "Yeah. Kind of."

Bingo-Bongo slapped his forehead. "Don't you know who she is? She's Mr. HahaFace's daughter!"

15

"Oh, wow." I sank onto the cot. "I didn't know. Do you think she'll get me in trouble?"

Bingo-Bongo rolled the phone around in his hand. "No. You're probably okay. She knows it's your first day. And you didn't say anything bad about Mr. HahaFace — did you?"

I swallowed. "Well . . . actually. I think I said he's some kind of freak. And I asked Deanna why everyone is so scared of him?"

Bingo-Bongo slapped his forehead again. "I don't believe you did that. What did she say?"

"Nothing," I replied. "She didn't have time to answer. You called me to come in. Do you think I'm in trouble?"

"Does a pig sleep in mud?"

I stared at him. "What does *that* mean? Yes or no? Come on — answer me. What does that mean?"

He tapped away on his phone and didn't look up.

That night, I tossed and turned on my narrow cot.

I was so happy and excited when I arrived at the circus. But now, worries spun through my mind, worries and fears. I thought about Deanna Banana and what I'd said about her father. Maybe she wouldn't tell him. Maybe she thought it was funny.

Or . . . maybe I'd have another knife tossed at my head.

And what about the knife? It had to be Deanna's knife, the knife she said was missing. Had someone tried to kill me only a few hours after I arrived?

No. No way. That was crazy. I tried to force that thought from my mind. If I didn't stop thinking this stuff, I'd never get to sleep.

But then there was Clown Street. And the Dunk-A-Klown booth with the clown who seemed to disappear.

So many dark mysteries here. A clown circus is supposed to be a happy place. Why was everyone so tense and mysterious?

I tried sleeping on one side. Then the other. Then on my back. But these troubling thoughts kept me wide awake.

I was finally starting to drift off to sleep when a sound made me sit up, alert again. A whisper. Outside the trailer window.

"Ray . . . Ray . . ."

At first, I thought it was the hiss of the trees across from the circus lot. But then I realized it had to be a person, someone whispering my name right outside the trailer.

"*Ray . . . Ray . . .*"

I scrambled to the window, pushed the blinds up, and peered outside. A full moon sent a yellow glow over the grass in front of the trailer.

I didn't see anyone.

"Who's there?" I called softly. A waste of time, since the window was closed.

In the cot across from mine, Bingo-Bongo groaned. I didn't call out again. I didn't want to wake him.

I peered through the blinds. All I could see was the glowing grass and the trailer across from ours, completely dark.

I turned away from the window. And heard the whispers again:

"*Ray . . . Ray . . .*"

The sound of my own name sent a cold chill to the back of my neck. I scrambled into jeans and a T-shirt and hurried out the trailer door.

"Whoa." The metal stairs felt cold on my bare feet. I stopped on the first step and glanced all around. The moonlight reflected off the trailers across from me. No one was in sight.

I lowered my foot to the second step — and

tripped. Tripped over something hard stretched across the stairs.

I let out a sharp cry as I stumbled. Both hands thrashed the air helplessly as I struggled to regain my balance. But I stumbled and fell, fell facedown into something soft and smelly.

"Oww." Pain shot through my body. I raised my head quickly. A sick, sour odor invaded my nostrils. I was lying in something disgusting, lumpy, and rotting.

Gagging on the horrible smell, I forced myself to my knees. And saw the pile of fish heads, fish guts, fish bones, and parts. The disgusting stuff stuck to the front of my T-shirt and the legs of my jeans.

I jumped up, brushing frantically with both hands.

Who did this?

I turned and saw the cord stretched across the trailer steps. My stomach lurching, I backed away, my feet squishing over the rotten fish guts.

Someone put that cord there to trip me. Someone scattered the disgusting fish parts in front of the stairs.

Someone wants to scare me. Or hurt me.

I scraped the bottoms of my feet on the grass. I knew I'd smell the putrid fish for days. I had to take a shower. But that wouldn't remove the sight or the smell from my mind.

I bent and untied the cord. I tossed it across the grass. Then I started up the stairs.

And as I reached the trailer door, I heard a chilling whisper from somewhere behind me:

"*Ray . . . Ray . . . Ray . . .*"

16

The next morning in the breakfast tent, Uncle Theo listened to my story. "Who would do that to me?" I demanded. "Why would someone want to hurt me?"

He patted my shoulder. "Circus clowns like to play tricks," he said. "Especially on new-comers."

"But, Uncle Theo —" I protested.

"It was smelly and gross," he said. "But it was just a joke. Don't take it personally."

"Huh? Don't take it personally?" I cried. "I'm going to smell like fish for the rest of my life!"

Uncle Theo had his eye on the tent entrance. "Mr. HahaFace just walked in," he said. He bumped my arm. "Go ahead. Eat your eggs. Don't draw his attention."

I watched the tall ringmaster in his red jacket with gold buttons up and down, and his top hat straight on his head. He wandered along the aisle between the tables. Once again, the food table got quiet.

Deanna Banana was eating breakfast by herself at the far end of a table. Mr. HahaFace sat down across from her, picked up a slice of bacon from her plate, and popped it into his mouth.

Uncle Theo bumped me again. "Come on. Finish your breakfast. We have a lot of rehearsing to do. We have to get you ready for your first show this afternoon."

I wasn't very hungry. I finished the scrambled eggs but left the potatoes and sausage on my plate.

I glanced down the table. Tommy Teardrops was sitting across from Bingo-Bongo. My roommate had a ping-pong paddle in his hand and was bouncing a ball against the tabletop.

The clowns were all in costume. It was Mr. HahaFace's rule that we all had to be in costume from morning to night.

I stood up. "Ready to go," I said.

Uncle Theo patted the pillow over my stomach. "That costume fits okay, Mr. Belly-Bounce." He studied me for a long moment. "But you can't wear those sneakers. Where are the clown shoes I gave you?"

"I forgot them," I said. "They're in the trailer. Want me to go back and get them?"

He adjusted the rubber snake around his neck. "No. No problem. We can rehearse without them."

As we started to leave, he slapped Tommy Teardrops hard on the back. Tommy spit his coffee across the table. Uncle Theo laughed. I could see he was getting into his Murder the Clown character.

I followed him into the show tent. The four men in the trapeze act were already practicing, swinging high, nearly at the top of the tent.

"They call themselves the Flying Fool Brothers," Uncle Theo said. "They're right about the *Fool* part. But they're not really brothers. They don't even look alike."

"Duck!" I heard a shout. "Duck!"

"Huh?" I gasped and ducked my head. I expected another knife to come whirling past me.

But no.

"Duck!" came the cry again. "Duck!"

I turned and saw Billy Laffs chasing a duck across the ring.

The duck honked and flapped its wings. Billy started to honk and flap his arms. The two of them made a complete circle around the ring.

"That's how he warms up in the morning," Uncle Theo said in his Murder the Clown voice. "I think the duck has all the talent. Billy Laffs

61

agrees with me. But he says when the act is over, he's still going to have a roasted duck dinner."

I laughed. I never knew when Uncle Theo was joking or telling the truth.

The Flying Fool Brothers were shouting overhead as they swung easily from trapeze to trapeze. In the center of the ring, four blue-uniformed workers were checking out the safety net.

Uncle Theo pulled me to a side of the tent where no one was rehearsing. "Okay, Mr. Belly-Bounce. I'm going to come walking toward you, my head in the air, minding my own business. I want you to bump me with your belly. Bump me hard. Make it funny."

"I'll try," I said. *Make it funny.*

He backed up to the tent entrance. Then he came walking toward me, swinging his arms, his big shoes kicking up the sawdust. His eyes were raised to the tent top, his head tilted back, moving from side to side.

I took a deep breath. Then I stuck my big pillow-belly out, stepped in front of him, and bumped him hard.

"Whooooaaah!" He let out a cry, threw his hands out, and pretended to stagger back. "Murder! That was murder!"

"How was it really?" I said.

"Not bad," he said. "But not good. Let me show you."

He backed up. Then he came charging at me. He bumped me with his stomach and sent me stumbling back against the tent wall.

"See?" he said. "You lower the pillow and bump *up* against the other person. Don't bump sideways. Bump from down to up. It looks funnier."

"Okay," I said. I *almost* understood what he was saying.

"Then, as soon as you've bumped me," he continued, "let out a loud cry and stagger back. You've got to be like a ball in a pinball machine. You bounce off me into someone else. You just keep bouncing. People will think it's a riot."

"Okay," I said.

"Let's try it again," he said. "And thrash your arms out. Make it look like you've completely lost your balance."

He strode back to the tent entrance, then came walking toward me again. I tried to remember everything he told me. I stepped in front of him and gave him a bump.

But no. Just as I dove forward, he dodged to the side. I missed and fell onto my stomach.

"Haw haw haw!" Murder burst out laughing. "Now *that's* funny!"

"You're about as funny as heat rash!" Billy Laffs told Murder.

"Have you looked in the mirror?" Murder shot back. "I've seen better-looking heat rash! Ha-ha!"

Billy Laffs held Murder by the shoulders. "The last time *you* looked in the mirror, the mirror shouted, 'I surrender!'"

"Hey, back off," my uncle said. "I'm trying to teach Mr. Belly-Bounce here how to be funny."

"That's like a whale trying to teach someone to fly!" Billy Laffs said.

"Remind me to laugh later," Murder said. "After I translate it into English!"

At the other side of the ring, I saw Deanna Banana enter. Her blond hair was all crazy around her face. She wore the same costume as when I met her the day before. She waved at me as she stepped into the ring, and I waved back.

She had an assistant with her, a skinny young man in short pants and a sleeveless white T-shirt. As I watched, he stood in front of a portable wall, and she threw knives at him.

He trembled and shook with each throw. That was his role. To shake and quake and shiver and act like he was terrified.

Deanna tossed knife after knife. Each one narrowly missed the shaking guy and sank into the wall behind him.

"Wow. I'm impressed," I said to Uncle Theo.

He nodded. "Yeah. She's good." He poked my belly with a finger. "Get back to work. You don't have time to stare at girls. You've got a lot to learn before the show this afternoon. Right now, you're like those fish guts you fell in last night. You *smell*! Ha-ha!"

I shuddered. "Please — don't remind me."

We practiced bumping and dodging for about half an hour. Then we practiced falling over backward and forward. By the time we went to the food tent for lunch, I was drenched in sweat right through my makeup.

I ate a big lunch. I'd really worked up an appetite from all that bumping and bouncing and falling down.

After lunch, I headed back to the trailer to rest. I didn't have much time. The show was at four. And I knew it would take me a long time to shower and do my clown makeup all over again, and get into my full costume.

The time went by in a blur. I guess I was more nervous than I thought I was. "Just have fun," Uncle Theo told me at lunch. "Just get out there and have fun. Then the audience will have fun, too."

It seemed like good advice. But I still felt a lot of pressure. I mean, think about it — my first time in a circus ring!

A little after three, Bingo-Bongo was getting dressed at one end of the trailer. And I was pulling on my Mr. Belly-Bounce costume at the other.

"Don't be nervous, kid," he said. "Just because hundreds of people will be watching your every move."

"Thanks a bunch," I said.

He laughed.

I straightened the red ruffle around my neck. Fixed the pillow in place. Then I bent to pick up my long, red, pointed clown shoes.

"Oh, nooooooo!" I let out a cry.

My clown shoes — someone had *sliced* them right down the middle.

17

I picked up the left shoe and examined it. The top of the shoe had been sliced, cut in a straight line. My hand was trembling. I dropped the shoe back to the trailer floor.

"Hey!" I called to Bingo-Bongo. "Is this some kind of joke you play on the new kid?"

He was facing the mirror, painting red circles on his cheeks. "Joke?" he said without turning around. "What kind of joke?"

"M-my shoes," I stammered. "Did you cut my shoes?"

He spun to face me. "Cut your shoes? Of course not. Why would I do that?"

I held them up to show him. "You didn't do it?"

He raised his right hand. "I swear to Bozo."

"Then who else was in our trailer?" My voice came out high and shrill.

He shrugged and turned back to the mirror.

I slid one of the shoes onto my foot. "They're

totally wrecked. How am I going to keep them on?" I said.

"Scotch tape, maybe?"

"You're a big help," I muttered. "Don't you care that someone sneaked into our trailer and sliced up my shoes? Probably the same someone who threw a knife at me and called me out of the trailer last night so I'd fall into a pile of rotting fish guts."

"That's crazy. Why would anyone do that to you?" Bingo-Bongo asked.

"That's what *I* want to know!" I cried. "Why?"

I stared hard at him. Did he know more than he was letting on?

The show started in the big tent at four o'clock. Mr. HahaFace strode into the spotlight in the center of the ring and, waving his top hat, he welcomed everyone.

The tent was jammed with hundreds of people. The clowns were all in a small backstage area. I peeked out at the crowd from behind the curtain flap.

My hands were sweaty. I could feel my heart doing acrobat flip-flops in my chest. Uncle Theo put a hand on my shoulder. "You'll be great," he said softly. "You've got the funny bones."

"I do?" I said. "I'm way nervous. Think I'll get a laugh if I go out there and puke my guts out?"

"Yes," he said. "That would *kill*. That would *murder* them!" He shook his head. "But you're not going to puke. You'll see. As soon as you get in the ring, you'll forget about being nervous. You'll only think about being funny."

He was right. When Mr. HahaFace blew his whistle and we clowns all came running into the ring, I felt a surge of energy shoot through my body. Like an electric shock.

I came roaring out full-speed and bounced off a pole. I heard people laugh — and that was it. I felt great. I bounced bellies with another clown and toppled onto my back. More laughs.

This is fun.

We clowns stood still as Murder the Clown stepped up to the seats. "What are you all staring at?" he bellowed. "I know I'm handsome — but that doesn't mean you have to stare!"

He grabbed the handle of the axe in his head. "I guess you're all staring at this, huh? How did I get it? Well, I got into a fight. Did I win the fight? Not really. I guess you'd call it a *split* decision! Ha-ha-ha!"

Murder asked for a volunteer for a water-spitting contest. "Let's see who would like a bath today!" he boomed.

He pulled a little redheaded boy from the first row. The boy looked really shy and afraid. Murder took a long drink from a big glass — and spit water all over the boy.

Then the boy surprised everyone. He grabbed the glass from his hand, took a long drink — and spit water all over Murder.

That got a huge roar from the crowd.

"Murder! I'll *murder* him!" my uncle bellowed. Murder chased him around the ring, and the boy went running back to his seat. Everyone went wild, cheering and laughing.

Deanna Banana took the center of the ring in her sparkly costume. She wheeled in a table stacked with knives. Once again, I watched her skinny assistant shake and quake as she threw knife after knife at him.

The audience gasped and oohed with each knife toss. The crowd loved her act. Each throw came close but missed. They roared with laughter at the end of her act. Her assistant turned around — and he had a knife in his *back*!

As she went running off, Mr. HahaFace blew his whistle again. That was the signal for the rest of us clowns to do our act, go crazy, fill the ring with stunts and gags.

I could feel the electric shock of excitement return as I darted into the ring, holding my big pillow belly high.

And guess what? That is when disaster struck.

As I neared the center of the ring, I tripped over Bingo-Bongo's shoes. My ruined clown shoes slipped off my feet. I stumbled — and sailed into Mr. HahaFace. He uttered a startled cry as I knocked him over — and landed heavily, on top of him.

The crowd loved it. But I could see by the scowl on his face that Mr. HahaFace didn't think it was funny.

I untangled myself from him and picked myself up. I bounced bellies with another clown and staggered around the ring.

For the rest of the performance, I could feel Mr. HahaFace's eyes on me. As I ran out of the ring at the end of the show, Uncle Theo shouted to me: "Good show! I told you — you've got the funny bones!"

But Mr. HahaFace stopped me at the tent flap. "I need to see you, Jack," he said. "Now!"

18

Mr. HahaFace grabbed the sleeve of my costume and pulled me from the tent. I nearly slipped out of my shoes again.

His face tight with anger, he led me away from the crowds leaving the tent. They all seemed happy, laughing and joking. It was easy to see that they enjoyed the show.

But the scowl on his face told me that the ringmaster was not happy.

The sun was dipping behind the tall trees across from the lot. A cool breeze felt good on my hot face. Somewhere nearby a cat was yowling.

Mr. HahaFace stopped at the side of the tent. He pressed his hands against his waist and glared at me. He didn't speak for the longest time. Finally, he said, "Jack, did you think barreling into me and knocking me on my butt was funny?"

I swallowed. My mouth was suddenly dry as cotton.

I wanted to say: *Yes. It got a really huge laugh. We should do it every show.*

But I'm not crazy.

I said, "Uh . . . well . . ."

"What put that stunt in your head?" the ringmaster demanded. "What on earth were you thinking, Jack?"

"My name is Ray, sir."

"Answer my question."

"Well . . . actually . . . it was an accident," I stammered.

He raised one eyebrow. "Accident?"

I nodded. "Yes. You see, I tripped over Bingo-Bongo's shoes and fell. I didn't really plan to knock you down."

He stared at me. I could see sweat forming on his forehead under the brim of his top hat. Finally, he said, "Bingo-Bongo tripped you? Is that what you're telling me?"

"No," I said. "He didn't trip me on purpose. I just fell. Because my shoes were loose. It wasn't his fault. Really."

He lowered his face till it was an inch from mine. "I see you're trying to protect Bingo-Bongo. He tripped you and —"

"No!" I insisted. "He didn't. I tripped over his shoes. That's all. He shouldn't be in trouble."

"Don't worry about Bingo-Bongo," Mr. HahaFace said. He made a shooing motion with both hands. He was finished with me. "Go rehearse falling on someone else, Jack."

I didn't wait around for him to say anything more. I turned and took off running. One of my ripped shoes slid off. I stopped to pick it up.

Some kids pointed at me and laughed. A little girl walked up to me. "Can I punch your big belly?" she asked.

I blinked. The question caught me by surprise. "Sure," I said.

She curled her little hand into a fist and punched my pillow stomach hard. I groaned and pretended to double over in pain. Actually, I didn't feel a thing. She laughed and went running back to her parents.

A small crowd had gathered. "What's your name?" a boy asked.

"Mr. Belly-Bounce."

"Is that your real stomach?"

"No," I said. "It's my clown stomach."

Two more kids wanted to punch it. They thought it was a riot.

Did I find it annoying? *No way.* I liked all the attention. And I liked making the kids laugh. Maybe my uncle was right. Maybe I really did have the funny bones.

The crowd had left the show tent. Now they

jammed the row of carnival games and food booths. My stomach growled.

I decided to get a hot dog or two before going back to my trailer. I turned toward the carnival booths — and someone stepped out to block my path.

Deanna Banana.

With a knife in her hand.

19

A chill of fear ran down my body. I started to step back.

But, whoa. Wait. It wasn't a knife in her hand. It was her phone.

She smiled. "Hey, how's it going?" She tucked her phone into her jacket pocket and walked up to me.

I let out a sigh of relief. Was I starting to lose it? Imagining things that weren't there? "Not bad," I said.

Her yellow jacket sparkled in the late afternoon sunlight. She wore the yellow pleated skirt and white tights that were her costume for the show. "Well, spill," she said. "How did your first show go? Did you enjoy it?"

I had the urge to tell her about tripping and knocking over Mr. HahaFace. But then I remembered he was her father. And I remembered I'd better be real careful around her.

"Awesome," I said. "I had a great time. I was surprised. I wasn't even nervous."

She nodded. Her eyes studied me for a long moment. Did she already know about how I messed up with her father? Was she waiting for me to tell her about it?

I kind of liked her. With her blond hair and blue eyes, she may have been the most awesome-looking girl I'd ever known. And she was the only one here at the circus who was my age.

But I knew I'd never be comfortable around her. I mean, I knew I'd always have to be on guard.

"I'm hungry," she said. "I'm always starving after a performance. Want to get some hot dogs?"

I laughed. "You read my mind. Definitely."

We began to walk side by side between the two rows of booths. It wasn't very crowded. People had seen the show. Now they were heading home to dinner.

Across from us, a little girl was struggling to hold a gigantic pink stuffed bear her father had won for her. The bear was actually as big as the little girl. People were still lined up at the cotton candy booth. And the *pop-pop-pop* didn't let up from the two rifle-firing ranges.

Past a dart-tossing booth, we came to a food cart with a sign: HOT DOGGIES. SO FRESH THEY'RE STILL BARKING.

A short, pudgy man in a white chef's hat and apron leaned forward to greet us. "Oh, hi, Deanna. How you doing?" he said. "Who's your big-bellied friend?"

"Hey, Uncle Noah," she said. She stood on tiptoes and leaned over the cart to kiss his cheek. "This is Ray. He's Theo's nephew."

Noah squinted at me. "Welcome to the circus, Ray. What'll you have? Two with everything?"

"Two with everything for both of us," Deanna said.

Noah turned to the grill.

"So do you know everyone who works here?" I asked.

Deanna nodded. "Pretty much. I grew up in the circus. A lot of the workers are my cousins and aunts and uncles."

"You never lived in a house?"

"No," she said. "Never. Only circus trailers."

"Weird," I said. "I've lived in the same house in Tampa my whole life."

"Well, I think *that's* weird," she said.

"I think you're both weird," her uncle Noah said. He handed us our hot dogs on paper plates. They were steaming hot, and the rolls bulged with sauerkraut, onions, mustard, and relish.

"How do I pay you?" I asked him. "I can't carry money in my clown suit. No pockets."

"That's what they *all* say," Noah joked. He

waved a hand. "You never have to pay if you're with Deanna."

We thanked him and walked on through the carnival, eating our hot dogs. Actually, we didn't *eat* them — we *devoured* them. Deanna was right. A circus show can make you seriously hungry.

At a game booth across from us, some kids were trying to toss basketballs into a high hoop. Next to them, I saw one of those old-fashioned Test-Your-Strength poles where you try to ring the bell at the top by slamming down a huge mallet.

"Want to try it?" Deanna asked.

"I don't think so," I said. "It's too easy."

She laughed.

We kept walking. I stopped when the Dunk-A-Klown tank came into view. I stopped and let out a cry. "Oh, no!"

"Keep walking." Deanna gave me a push. "Come on, Ray. Don't look. Just keep walking."

20

Deanna grabbed me by the arms and tried to pull me down the aisle. But I tugged myself free and turned to the tall water tank.

"Stay away," she warned. "Come on, Ray. You don't want to watch."

But I *had* to watch. Because it was Bingo-Bongo perched on the chair above the water.

He sat tensely, staring down at the crowd in front of the tank. He had his arms crossed tightly in front of him. I waved to him, but he didn't see me.

He was concentrating on the tall, powerful-looking man who had a stack of baseballs in his arms. I could see Bingo-Bongo's whole body trembling. He looked totally terrified.

"Come on, Ray," Deanna urged. "We don't have to watch this."

But I didn't move. The big man heaved a baseball at the target. Missed. Heaved another one. Missed.

His third throw hit the target with a loud *smack*.

The chair collapsed under Bingo-Bongo, and he dropped into the water tank, splashing water on the glass walls. His hands flew up as he dropped. He sank to the bottom, then started to swim.

Deanna gripped my arm tightly. She tried to pull me away.

But I refused to budge. I stared into the tank as Bingo-Bongo struggled to swim. His eyes bulged as he saw me. His face moved closer to the glass tank wall. He reached out with both hands, as if begging me to help him.

His lips moved. His mouth formed the words *help me.*

And as I stared, frozen in horror, he was flushed out of sight.

My heart pounding, I turned to Deanna. "We've got to *do* something!" I cried. "We've got to help him."

"We can't," she replied. "Don't you understand? He's being punished."

I swallowed. "Punished? But . . . but he'll be okay. Right?"

She squinted at me. "I've got to go," she said. She spun away from me and started to hurry off.

"No. Wait —" I started after her. "He'll be okay — right? Answer my question. He'll be okay?"

She didn't answer. Instead, she started running through the row of carnival booths. She almost collided with a baby stroller and then pushed her way through a group of teenagers.

"What was *that* about?" I murmured.

Why couldn't she answer a simple question?

I'll have to ask Bingo-Bongo where he went when he was flushed from the tank, I told myself.

I turned and started to head to our trailer. I kept seeing the look of horror on Bingo-Bongo's face. And his lips forming the words *help me.*

And then the frightening thought popped into my brain: *Was Bingo-Bongo being punished because of* me*? Because Mr. HahaFace thought he tripped me?*

No. Oh, please — no. Please don't let it be my fault.

The sun was nearly down. The sky was a solid charcoal gray. The lights came on all over the circus lot. White lights, also red and blue. So many lights, it almost looked bright as day.

The air still felt heavy and humid. I couldn't wait to get out of the clown suit and take a shower. I had to hurry back to the trailer and see if Bingo-Bongo was already back.

I still hadn't completely learned my way around. The trailers at the far end of the lot all looked alike. They were parked at odd angles, which made it hard to remember which was mine.

After circling the trailers twice, I finally found mine and started eagerly to the door. To my surprise, the ping-pong table that Bingo-Bongo kept out front was gone. I wondered why he had moved it.

I saw a light inside through the trailer window. I guessed he'd beaten me back to the trailer.

I pushed open the door and called out, "Hey — are you home?"

No answer.

I stepped into the trailer and waited for my eyes to adjust to the dim light. The first thing I noticed was that the food counter in our kitchen area was bare.

Weird, I thought. Bingo-Bongo used to have his nacho chip bags and candy bars and cookie boxes all over the place. Why had he cleaned up?

Bingo-Bongo's big black trunk was gone. And the framed photograph of his dog back home had been removed from the wall.

I heard a cough. I turned — and saw someone sitting on Bingo-Bongo's cot. "Hey, you're here!" I cried. "You're back. Wow. Thank goodness!"

The clown turned to face me. He had a red bulb nose and a thick stubble of beard, a funny little red top hat angled over his black hair. His costume was white with red stripes.

"Hi," he said. He had a funny, squeaky voice.

"Who are you?" I asked.

He climbed up from the cot, crossed the trailer, and stuck out his hand for me to shake. "I'm Dr. Phooey," he said. "Who are you?"

"Uh . . . Ray," I answered. "Well, actually, Mr. Belly-Bounce."

He nodded. "Nice to meet you. I took that bunk against the wall. Is that okay?"

I stared hard at him. "Yeah. But that's Bingo-Bongo's cot," I said. "Where is he? Where did he go?"

Dr. Phooey gave a sad shrug. "Poor guy. I heard he went to Clown Street."

A stab of fear made me gasp. I felt my heart skip a beat.

Dr. Phooey gave another sad shrug, his eyes half-closed. He walked back to his cot and sat down.

I followed and sat across from him on my cot. "You have to tell me about Clown Street," I said. "You have to tell me."

"What is there to tell?" he replied.

"Where is it? Why is it such a bad place?" I demanded. "Why doesn't anyone want to talk about it?"

The clown leaned forward and spoke in a low voice. "I just got here. I need this job. I have to keep my nose clean. Know what I mean?"

"Just tell me what Clown Street is!" I insisted.

"Listen, kid. Ray. Whatever you said your name is. Do what they tell you. You won't have any trouble. You're just a kid. You don't have to worry about things like that."

He had his eyes on the trailer window. Like he thought someone might be outside spying on us.

"Be a clown," he said. "Be happy."

He climbed to his feet. He brushed off the front of his costume with both hands. Then he started to the door.

"I don't get it," I said. "Why won't you answer a simple question?"

"I've got to go pick up my trunk," he said. "Catch you later, dude." He disappeared out the door.

"So what is Clown Street?" I said out loud to myself. "Why won't anyone tell me?"

I sat hunched on my cot with my hands clasped in front of me. I gazed around the trailer. All of Bingo-Bongo's stuff was gone. Everything had been taken away. And ... *he* had been taken away.

A heavy feeling of dread made me feel sick to my stomach. Was it my fault? Had Mr. HahaFace sent Bingo-Bongo to Clown Street because he thought he tripped me and made me knock HahaFace over?

How crazy was that?

But was it true?

Leaning forward on my cot, I felt my stomach do flip-flops. My hands were suddenly cold and sweaty.

It was only my second day at the circus. But I

was already convinced this was not a happy place. In fact, this was a *dangerous* place.

In my mind, I replayed what had happened to me since I arrived. The knife that barely missed my head. The whispered voice calling my name outside the trailer at night, and the pile of fish guts in front of the steps. My clown shoes, slashed in half . . .

Someone was trying to tell me something. Someone was trying to scare me.

Everyone seemed scared at this circus. Scared of Mr. HahaFace. Scared of going to Clown Street. And now, my roommate was gone. Could that mean that I'd be next?

I had to find out the answers to all my questions. And I knew one person who could answer them all. Uncle Theo.

I jumped to my feet. I really wanted to get out of this costume. But I was desperate to talk to my uncle. I kicked off the ruined clown shoes and pulled on my sneakers. Then I hurried out of the trailer.

Night now. The carnival booths were closed. The people had all gone home. I saw a few clowns making their way to the food tent for dinner. But I wasn't hungry. I knew I couldn't eat until I had forced Uncle Theo to tell me everything.

Deanna's trailer was dark. Maybe she was at the food tent, too. I decided Uncle Theo was probably there.

An early dew had formed. My sneakers squished over the wet grass. I strode past the show tent. The lights were on inside. I saw some blue-uniformed workers on tall ladders, adjusting the big sound speakers.

Two cats were prowling around the garbage cans at the side of the food tent. One of them knocked a lid over. It hit the ground, and the two cats took off in different directions, as if a bomb had gone off.

I stepped into the food tent and gazed up and down the tables for Uncle Theo. It must have been pizza night, because I saw big plates of pepperoni pizza in front of everyone.

Billy Laffs waved at me and motioned for me to come sit down. But I shook my head and shouted, "Have you seen my uncle Theo?"

"Not since the performance," he called back. "He stunk up the show. He's probably ashamed to show his face."

He saw that I didn't laugh. I wasn't in a laughing mood.

"Hey — just kidding," he called. "Just clowning. It's a job, you know."

"I'll try his mobile home," I said.

The pizza aroma followed me as I walked out of the tent and took the path toward my uncle's little house. Behind me in the tent, I heard Mrs. Giggle-Wiggle laughing. Some clowns were arguing over the best way to do a water spit.

They seem happy, I thought. *You'd never guess that something is terribly wrong here.*

The lights were on in Uncle Theo's mobile home. I knocked on the door, then let myself in. "Uncle Theo? Are you here?"

"In the back," he shouted.

I stepped through the short hallway and stopped at the door to the bedroom. Uncle Theo sat at his dressing table, his back to me. In the mirror in front of him, I could see he was removing his clown makeup.

"Hi. It's me," I said.

He didn't turn around. "How's it going?" he asked. He quickly lowered his head.

"I . . . I wanted to talk to you," I stammered. "I'm worried and I thought —"

He stopped wiping the thick greasepaint from his face and kept his head down. I watched him in the mirror. "Tell me what you're worried about," he said.

But I didn't answer him. I couldn't speak. I opened my mouth in a gasp of horror.

I stared into the mirror, frozen in disbelief. Frozen in shock.

The man sitting there in front of me . . . the man who stopped removing his Murder the Clown makeup . . .

He wasn't my uncle Theo.

23

My heart thudded so loud I could hear it. I took a step closer.

I blinked several times. Maybe I was wrong. Maybe the dim light of the room made him appear different. Maybe I was seeing things.

But no. I could see his face in the mirror clearly. It wasn't my uncle's face. The eyes were closer together. The nose was longer and came to a point. The chin . . .

No. No! Not my uncle!

Finally, my silence made him turn around. He dropped the cotton pad he was using to remove the makeup. His eyes met mine.

"Ray . . ." the man murmured. "Listen to me . . ."

I didn't move. I stared at his thinning, short hair. The small dark eyes. Not Uncle Theo's eyes.

"Where is he?" I managed to choke out. "Where is my uncle?"

"Ray —"

"Who *are* you?" I screamed.

"I'm really sorry," the man said. He motioned for me to sit down on the tall stool next to his dressing table.

But I didn't move. I stood stiffly, my arms crossed tightly in front of me.

"I ... didn't want to ruin your summer," he stammered. He shook his head. "I thought maybe I could fool you. For a while, at least. I know you came here for fun, and I didn't want to spoil that."

His voice broke on the words. I could see he was telling the truth. I could see he was very upset. His hands trembled so hard, he gripped the edge of the makeup table.

"Where is my uncle?" I repeated.

"He's not here, Ray," he replied. He kept his eyes locked on me. "He wrote that letter to you. Inviting you to the circus for the summer. But ... but ..."

Again, his voice broke.

He took a deep breath. "Right after he wrote to you, he got in trouble with Mr. HahaFace. Bad trouble. And Mr. HahaFace sent him to Clown Street."

A long sigh escaped my throat. Uncle Theo was at Clown Street? What did that mean?

The man drummed his fingers tensely on the tabletop. "My real name is David Ford," he said softly. "My clown name is Monkey Face, because

I can make a hundred funny faces. I was a friend of your uncle's."

As he spoke, I lowered my arms. I crossed the room and sat down on the tall stool beside him.

"Mr. HahaFace called me into his office," he continued. "He told me about Theo being sent away. He said I had to be Murder the Clown from then on."

I gasped. "He told you to take over my uncle's clown act? But Uncle Theo told me he created that clown. He worked as Murder his whole career."

"I know," David said. "That's what I told HahaFace. But he said he would send me to Clown Street, too, if I didn't take over as Murder the Clown. And he ordered me not to tell you the truth. He knew you were coming. He ordered me to keep my makeup on around you and let you think I was your uncle."

I stared hard at him. This whole thing was hard to believe. No. It was *impossible* to believe.

But I believed him.

He reached out and patted the back of my hand. "I'm so sorry, Ray," he said. "I had no choice."

I jumped down off the stool. "I have to find my uncle," I said.

"No. You can't," he cried. "Don't even think about it."

"Where is Clown Street, David? How do I get to Clown Street?"

"Y-you can't," he stuttered. "You can't go there. It's too late."

"I have to try to find him," I insisted. "I have to try to save him — and Bingo-Bongo, too."

"No. It's too dangerous. Trust me. It can't be done."

"Well, I'm doing it!" I cried.

I spun away from him. My legs felt like rubber bands, but I forced myself to stagger out of his mobile home.

I heard him shouting behind me. But I ignored him.

I ran out into the night. Heavy, humid air. A tiny sliver of a moon low in the black sky. Lights twinkling over the circus grounds.

I ran toward the show tent. No one in sight. The tent was dark and empty inside. I nearly stumbled over a cat, prowling across the grass. Probably hunting for food.

I have my own hunting to do, I thought. *I have to find Clown Street.*

But how could I get there? How could I save Uncle Theo and Bingo-Bongo?

Suddenly, I figured it out.

24

The name Clown Street sounded like a happy place. But now I knew the truth. I knew it was a dangerous, frightening place. That's why the clowns never wanted to talk about it. They lived in terror of being sent there.

Mr. HahaFace, the ringmaster, was the one who sent them there. If you made him angry, if you did something he didn't like, he sent you to Clown Street. And you never returned.

Was Uncle Theo still alive? Why did David Ford say it was too late to rescue him?

I didn't care. I had to try.

I pictured Mr. HahaFace, and my chest suddenly burned with anger. He was supposed to be a clown. How could he be so evil? Did he enjoy having the power? The power to make everyone in the circus afraid of him? The power to send clowns away forever?

These questions flamed through my mind. I found myself trotting toward Mr. HahaFace's mobile home on the other side of the lot. And each step I took made my anger grow.

My hands balled into tight fists. I swung them at my sides as I ran. My whole body burned with my anger.

I pictured myself punching HahaFace. Punching him in the face. Punching him with both fists . . . till he told me how to rescue my uncle.

As I passed a clump of trailers at the edge of the lot, a better plan started to come to me.

I have to get to Clown Street.

The only one who can send me there is Mr. HahaFace.

I have to do something that will make Mr. HahaFace eager to send me there. I have to do something that will anger him enough to send me to Clown Street immediately.

What could I do?

My brain was spinning as I reached the carnival area. The booths were all lighted by the white, red, and blue lights strung above them. But no one was in sight.

Three or four night birds fought over scraps of food that had been tossed on the ground. No other sign of life.

I started to walk past the carnival. But a booth caught my eyes. A bakery booth at the near end. Were those pies in the display case?

I turned and trotted over to the booth. Despite the heat of the night, my skin felt tingly and cold.

I gazed into the refrigerator case at the side of the booth. Yes. The case was filled with pies. I saw fruit pies and a cream pie on the bottom shelf.

Suddenly, I knew how to get HahaFace to send me to Clown Street. No problem.

Was the glass case unlocked? Yes. I pulled open the door, stooped down, and carefully slid out the cream pie. I stuck a finger into the whipped cream top and tasted it.

Sweet.

I balanced the pie in one hand and continued my trip across the lot. Mr. HahaFace's little mobile home stood all by itself between two tall evergreen shrubs. A yellow front-porch light sent a rectangle of light over the door.

I took a deep breath and walked closer. It was a terrifying moment, but my anger kept me moving. I held the pie steady in front of me.

I planned to knock on the door. When Mr. HahaFace opened it, I'd smash the cream pie as hard as I could into his face.

The dude already disliked me because I knocked him over in the ring. The pie would definitely make him hate me enough to send me to Clown Street.

My legs were trembling like crazy. But I forced myself to climb onto the front stoop. I held the pie high in one hand — and raised my other hand to knock on the front door.

25

My hand hung in the air for a few seconds. Then I lowered it to my side.

There were no lights on inside. The front window was completely black.

Mr. HahaFace must be asleep.

"Maybe that's even better," I murmured to myself.

If I wake him up with a cream pie in the face, he'll be even angrier. He'll be so furious, he'll send me to Clown Street in less than a minute.

My hand shook as I gripped the doorknob. I turned it and pushed. No. I tried pulling. No. The front door was locked.

Under the yellow porch light, I turned my eyes to the window beside the stoop. Behind the screen, it was open about one-third of the way.

Was it big enough for me to slip inside? Yes.

I set the pie down and tiptoed to the window. It took me a few minutes to remove the screen. I tossed it onto the grass.

Then I used both hands to push the window all the way up. Cold air escaped through the opening. Mr. HahaFace must have had the air conditioning cranked up high.

I carefully lifted the pie and carried it to the open window. Then I lowered one leg into the house. Holding the pie in two hands, I lowered my other leg over the window ledge.

I stood for a long moment in the darkness, waiting for my heartbeat to slow down and my breathing to return to normal. Pale moonlight washed into the room.

I was standing in a small living room. A couch faced a flat screen TV on one wall. A table held a stack of newspapers and magazines.

I waited for my eyes to adjust. The room smelled smoky and stale. The air was sour. Did Mr. HahaFace smoke cigars?

A back hallway came into focus. I guessed that the bedroom was at the end of that hall. Balancing the pie in front of me with one hand, I stepped into the hallway.

My foot knocked over something on the floor. A bottle? It clanked as it rolled in front of me. I held my breath and listened.

Did that wake HahaFace up?

Silence.

Still holding my breath, I crept as carefully as I could toward the end of the narrow hall. A doorway stood on the right. It had to be his bedroom door. The door was open. The room was pitch-black.

I took a step into the bedroom.

A wave of panic swept over me, making my whole body shudder.

Was this a crazy thing to do?

Of *course* it was. But if it worked . . . if it made him send me to Clown Street . . . it was worth being scared out of my mind.

Hazy gray light poured in from the bedroom window. I narrowed my eyes at the bed against the wall, struggling to see clearly. I could hear him snoring softly. Despite the warm night, the covers were pulled up to his chin.

He was sleeping on his back. His mouth hung open as he snored.

Again, I held my breath. I took a silent step toward the bed. Then another. Another.

Now I stood above him. I didn't hesitate. I raised the pie in one hand, raised it high . . .

. . . and smashed it into his sleeping face.

26

It made a loud *squish* as the whipped cream and pie filling spread over his face. He uttered a long, loud groan.

I jumped back. My heart skipped a beat.

The whipped cream covered his eyes, his nose, his mouth. He sat straight up and groaned again. He shook his head hard, like a dog after a bath. Then he raised both hands and swiped at his face. He cleared the whipped cream from his nose with his fingers, then his eyes.

I stood frozen like a statue. *Did I really do this?*

He blew hard, sending whipped cream flying from his mouth. The pie oozed onto the front of his nightshirt. He groaned again.

Finally, he looked up and spotted me standing beside the bed. He blinked. He used the sheet to wipe more pie off his face. Pie covered the front of his nightshirt. It puddled over his covers.

"Ray?" His voice was still choked with sleep. A blob of whipped cream clung to his forehead and eyebrows.

I pressed my hands against my sides and tried to stop shaking.

"Ray? Is that you?" He kept blinking, squinting at me.

My stomach did a flip-flop. I had a sudden feeling something had gone terribly wrong. My brain was too scrambled to figure it out.

"Ray?" His hand fumbled against the wall. He found a light switch and clicked it on.

Then, wiping pie from his hair, he turned to face me. He dropped his feet to the floor and stood up.

And that's when I realized what had gone wrong.

"Tommy Teardrops!" I cried. "Oh, wow. Oh, no. Wh-where is Mr. HahaFace?"

The wrong clown. I had just pied Tommy Teardrops.

"Did you mean to deliver this pie to HahaFace?" Tommy asked.

"Yes. I'm sorry," I said. "I never meant to do it to you. I didn't know —"

Tommy Teardrops crossed the room and picked up a towel from the dresser top. He wiped his face and head with it.

He licked some pie off his upper lip. "Not bad, kid. Is it banana cream?"

"I'm really sorry," I repeated.

He shrugged. "Well ... I usually like to eat my pie when I'm *awake* — not sound asleep."

"I thought you were Mr. HahaFace," I said. "Really."

"He's away tonight," Tommy explained. He used the towel to work pie out of his ears. "HahaFace is staying in town with some friends. So I slept here because my trailer is broken. A leaky water pipe."

"Oh, wow," I murmured. "Oh, wow."

Tommy's eyes flashed. "Did Mr. HahaFace *know* you were coming with a pie tonight? He didn't tell me to expect you."

I shook my head. "No. He didn't know. I wanted to surprise him."

Tommy squinted at me. "And you did it *because* ...?"

I hesitated. I didn't want to tell Tommy Teardrops my plan. I knew he wouldn't understand. He wouldn't help me get to Clown Street. He'd try to stop me.

"It ... it was just a joke," I lied.

Tommy squinted at me. "A joke? Really? Ray, that kind of joke could get you a one-way trip to Clown Street."

"That's what I want!" I blurted out. "Don't you see? I have to help my uncle. I have to find Uncle Theo and get him out of wherever he is."

Tommy shook his head sadly. "It's too late,

103

Ray. Don't try it. I liked your uncle. He was a good guy. But it's too late."

"I have to try," I said. I turned and started toward the door.

"No one ever returns from Clown Street!" he shouted after me.

I stopped at the front door. "I'll be the first," I called back. "Me and Uncle Theo. I'm going there now, Tommy."

And as I closed the door behind me and stepped out into the hot summer night, I realized exactly how to get there. I took a deep breath. Then I took off running to the Dunk-A-Klown tank.

The Dunk-A-Klown tank *had* to be the way to get to Clown Street.

I suddenly felt like an idiot. Trying to make Mr. HahaFace angry was a total waste of time. What a stupid idea that had been.

I pictured the clowns who had been perched on the seat in the water tank. And I remembered their faces, so frightened. Terrified.

Bingo-Bongo was shaking in fear when he sat above the tank. And when the water flushed and sank from the tank, he frantically tried to stay afloat.

I watched as he vanished, sucked into the bottom of the tank. He must have been flushed to Clown Street. The water must have swept him to wherever that street is located.

My shoes thudded the wet grass as I ran full-speed to the carnival area. Under the sparkling lights, the booths glowed eerily. Empty. Like a ghost town.

I ran past the bakery booth with the missing cream pie in the display case. In the balloon dart game booth, the giant teddy bear prizes stared blankly at me as I passed.

A gust of wind rattled the flags over the Chicken-On-A-Stick booth. The wind made whistling sounds as it swept through the carnival. Balloons shook and booth walls creaked.

The Dunk-A-Klown tank came into view. The water looked dark and deep. The surface rolled and splashed in the sudden wind gusts.

I stared at the chair high above the water. Once again, I pictured Bingo-Bongo up there, hugging himself, his face twisted in fear, his whole body shaking.

I'm coming, I thought. *I'll save you, too.*

Breathing hard, sweat pouring down my forehead, I stepped up to the tank. I pressed my face against the glass and peered down.

The glass felt cool against my hot forehead. Inside, I could see the drain. It was closed, of course. Covered by a metal lid.

But I could see the drain clearly. Square and big enough for a person to fall through. Big enough to pull a person down . . . down to wherever the water led.

I took a step back. So how was this going to work? I had to climb behind the tank, then jump into the water. I had to dive to the bottom and pull the lid up — and let myself be flushed down the drain.

I can do this, I told myself.

I turned and walked to the side of the water tank. I grabbed the ladder tilted there and raised a foot to the lowest rung. That's when I saw someone step quickly out of the deep shadows.

She ran toward me and pulled me from the ladder.

"Don't!" Deanna shouted.

"You're not going to stop me," I cried. "No way!"

28

"You can't do this, Ray," she said.

Her blond hair was pulled back in a tight ponytail. Her eyes locked on mine. She wore a white tank top pulled down over dark straight-legged jeans.

"Get back, Ray," she said. "I know what you're doing, and it's crazy."

"Go away, Deanna," I insisted. "I know who you are. I know you are Mr. HahaFace's daughter. And I know you have been spying for him. But I'm not going to let you stop me. I'm serious. I —"

"Shut up," she snapped. Her expression turned cold. "You don't understand anything."

"I understand that my uncle is in trouble," I said. "And I'm going to find him. I'm going in this tank. You're not going to stop me." I lowered my shoulder and tried to push past her.

But she grabbed my shoulder and whirled me

around. "Stop! Stop! You don't understand. I'm on *your* side!" she screamed.

I was panting hard. I squinted at her. "What?"

"I'm on your side," she repeated.

Another gust of hot wind made waves roll at the surface of the water tank. The wind howled down the wide aisle between the carnival booths.

I shook my head hard, trying to clear it. Was Deanna telling the truth?

She stood almost nose to nose with me, with her hands pressed against her waist. "I've been trying to warn you all along," she said. "I've been trying to warn you to go home. This circus is *evil*."

"But — I —" My mouth hung open. She was Mr. HahaFace's daughter. Why was she saying that?

"I threw the knife past your head on the day you arrived," Deanna said. "I whispered your name and made you fall into the smelly fish guts. That was *me*, Ray. And I cut your clown shoes in two."

"Huh?" My mouth still hung open. "You did all that to *help* me? Are you crazy?!"

"I did all that to *warn* you," she insisted. "And I'm warning you now —"

I didn't know whether to be angry or . . . or *what*? I couldn't believe Deanna thought it was a good idea to do those things to me.

I pushed her shoulders against the tank. "Do you want to help me?" I said through gritted teeth. "Seriously? Do you want to help me? Then don't throw knives at me. Help me get to my uncle Theo."

She ducked out of my grasp. She shoved me back. "I can't let you go there, Ray. No one ever comes back from Clown Street. No one."

I scowled at her and spun away. I strode quickly to the ladder at the side of the tank. The ladder led up to the chair perched high over the water.

"No — Ray!" Deanna chased after me. "You don't want to do this. My father . . . he . . . he sent a lot of clowns there. I never saw them again."

I ignored her. I pulled myself up the ladder. "Maybe I'm crazy," I called down to her. "My parents say I do crazy things all the time. But there's *no way* I'm going to leave my uncle out there. No way."

I hoisted myself onto the chair. I gazed down at the water. It was dark green under the pale moonlight and the twinkling carnival lights. Despite the hot night, I shivered. I held on to the seat of the little chair with both hands.

"Come on, Deanna," I called. "Help me."

She stood at the side of the tank, arms crossed, staring up at me. "Ray, I don't want you to do this."

"Help me," I said again. "See those baseballs on the table? Get them, Deanna. Start throwing them."

"No," she insisted. "It's too dangerous. It's too impossible."

"Throw the baseballs," I said. "Help me do this." I let go of the seat and motioned with both hands. "Come on. Hit the target. Send me into the water."

From all the way up in the chair, I heard her sigh. She shook her head. I could see she was thinking hard, trying to decide what to do.

Finally, she picked up four or five baseballs and held them in her arms. "I don't like this," she said. "But I'll try to help you."

"Come on," I shouted. "Throw them. Hit the target. Pretend you're throwing a knife."

She pulled back her arm and tossed a baseball. It missed the target by a mile. It hit the back wall and bounced into the water.

I gripped the seat bottom again. How crazy was this? Was I sending myself to my own doom?

I tried to force all those questions from my mind. I held on to my little perch and stared at the target.

Deanna threw again. Missed.

I could hear her muttering unhappily to herself. As a knife-thrower, she never missed.

Another toss. Missed the target by less than an inch.

111

"So close!" I cried. "Come on — one more. The next one will get it!"

Sure enough, I was right.

The hard ball made a *smack* sound as it hit the target dead center. The sharp sound rang in my ears.

I held my breath as my chair collapsed, and I went sliding down. I dropped into the tank with a loud *splash*. High waves of water rose up around me.

Shuddering from the shock of the sudden cold, I quickly sank to the bottom.

29

I opened my eyes but could see only dark green water all around me. I fought the urge to struggle to the surface. Instead, I hunched my body and forced myself to stay at the bottom.

Above me, I heard the hum of machinery. I saw the drain on the tank floor lift up. And a few seconds after that, I felt the strong pull of the water as it began to pour into the drain.

I forced my body to go limp. I felt the strong current washing over me, pulling me down. I didn't try to fight it.

A few seconds later, I was tugged into the open hole. The drain was just wide enough for my body to slip through. The current was powerful, pulling me down with great force. I knew I couldn't fight it even if I wanted to.

I sank into total darkness. The raging water seemed to carry me into a deeper and deeper black. I landed on my back. I realized I was on a steep water slide that carried me down . . . down.

The slide tilted up. Carried by the powerful current, I was being carried sideways through the intense darkness. Still underwater, my chest began to ache.

Was I going to drown in this tunnel?

I shot around a curve, then slid straight ahead. It seemed as if I'd been sliding for hours. But that was impossible.

My head was spinning. Rays of bright red flashed in front of my eyes. My chest felt about to explode.

Can't breathe . . . Can't breathe down here . . .

Hold it in, Ray . . .

And then the raging stream lifted me up. My head shot above the surface. Still sliding through darkness, I gasped in breath after breath.

The water bubbled around me, sending hard waves over my body. The current seemed to grow even more powerful. A rushing waterfall carrying me . . . *where?*

I could hear only the endless rush of the water as it carried me along the slide. I could see only the black walls of the tunnel.

Did it stretch on for miles?

I choked on a mouthful of the cold water. Gagging and spitting, I struggled to regain my breath.

Suddenly, the slide angled down sharply. My body dipped with it. Again, I felt like I was falling, falling into the watery blackness.

And then . . . gray light.

I bobbed to the surface. Blinking away water, I glimpsed light all around me. I spun in a circle, gasping for breath. I kicked my legs to make sure they still worked.

The current stopped. The surface of the water flattened out.

"Where am I?" I murmured out loud.

Squinting into the gray light, I started to swim. My arms felt heavy and weak. But I forced them to pull me over the water.

Was I in a lake? A wide river?

I raised my eyes and saw a dark, flat surface stretching high above me.

I swam a bit farther, taking long, steady strokes.

"OW!" I uttered a cry as my head struck something hard.

I reeled back. I raised my hands in front of me — and rubbed them over a smooth, clear wall. A glass wall.

I'm in another water tank. A really huge tank.

I began to swim along the tank wall, keeping one hand on the glass. I turned a corner and kept swimming.

I couldn't see anything on the other side of the glass. Just the blank gray light.

This tank is big, I told myself. *But there has to be a way out.*

I turned another corner and kept swimming. I

couldn't remember if I'd made a complete circle or not.

I lowered my arms and treaded water for a moment, waiting to catch my breath. And that's when a strong hand gripped my shoulder from behind.

30

I let out a startled cry and whirled around.

"Deanna!" I cried. "I . . . I don't understand. What are you doing here?"

She bobbed on the surface, water running off her blond hair. She raised both hands and wiped water off her face. "I had to follow you," she said. "I couldn't let you go alone."

I shook my head in disbelief. "Are you crazy?"

"We both are," she said. She glanced around. "Where are we?"

"Some kind of water tank," I said. "That's all I can figure out."

"Do you see a way out of here?"

I shook my head. And then I felt the water start to move around us. It came rushing at us like a tidal wave and splashed hard against the tank wall. And then, another hard splash against the glass. The water tumbled and rocked.

Gazing over Deanna's shoulders, I saw something move under the water. Something dark . . .

and big. Big enough to rumble all the water in the tank.

"Deanna," I tapped her shoulder. "Better turn around."

And now, we were both facing the enormous THING as it pulled itself up from the water. We pressed our backs against the glass tank wall and stared in horror.

"Is it a *plant*?" I cried.

I saw long, pulsing tendrils curling from its sides. But the middle of the big thing squeezed in, then out — *as if it was breathing*!

And when I saw the gaping mouth pull open on the front of its bulb-like head and saw the rows of huge, jagged teeth — I knew it wasn't a plant.

"It's some kind of mutant squid!" Deanna cried, squeezing my shoulder. "It's a GIANT MUTANT squid!"

"I . . . I don't think it's friendly," I muttered.

I watched, frozen in terror, as it roared up from the water. It stretched its tentacles toward us, reaching for us. And dove forward, lunging at us with surprising speed.

It splashed up wave after wave as it slid across the tank toward Deanna and me.

Deanna and I had our backs pressed against the tank wall. Nowhere to run. I raised both arms to shield myself. But the huge creature dove at me and covered me like a slimy, cold blanket.

It pressed me flat against the tank wall. I could feel its heart pulsing under its heavy slab of a body. I tried to duck beneath it. But there was no room.

And then I started to twist and squirm with all my might as the giant squid's tentacles wrapped around me. It gnashed its beak and pushed harder. The tentacles squeezed around my middle like tight, wet ropes. And then I felt them wrap around my legs.

I couldn't kick. I couldn't strike out with my arms. I couldn't breathe.

Tighter . . . tighter . . . The tentacles squeezed around my body.

Behind the creature, I saw Deanna struggling to free me. She punched the back of its head. Then she struggled to pull a tentacle from around my waist.

Her efforts became more frantic as she saw she wasn't strong enough. The squid was a *monster*, and I was the monster's victim.

I couldn't breathe. I couldn't move. My chest felt about to explode. I shut my eyes. My strength was draining . . . draining away.

I'm sorry, Uncle Theo, I thought. My last thought. *I'm sorry. I never even got to Clown Street.*

31

The tentacles jerked, then suddenly loosened. I opened my eyes.

I saw Deanna raise a knife to the creature's back. She must have had one of the knives from her circus act. She lowered the blade to the fleshy back.

The tentacles instantly unwrapped and slid away from me. They all flew up at once as the enormous creature retreated. It turned heavily, sending up another high wave of water, and plunged away from us, the knife still in its back.

I couldn't hold my breath any longer. I raised both arms and kicked hard, and pulled myself to the surface of the water. Then I gasped in breath after breath of the steamy air.

My chest ached. My whole body throbbed. Even though the squid was gone, I could still feel the slimy-hard tentacles around my chest and waist.

Deanna rose to the surface behind me, spitting water, breathing hard.

I turned to thank her, but I didn't get a chance.

I heard applause. Yes. People clapping. Laughter and applause.

"What on earth—?" I cried. I slapped the side of my head to clear water from my ears. Was I hearing things?

No. Peering through the glass wall of the tank, I saw faces. People sitting in rows of seats, staring at the tank. "An audience!" I cried to Deanna, pointing. "Look. Those people were watching us."

She shook water off her face. Tugged back her ponytail. Stared through the glass. "They watched us fight that squid?"

Shadows fell over the sides of the tank. I turned and saw two grinning clowns in red-and-white ruffled costumes. They leaned over the sides of the tank and motioned for us to swim to them.

The clowns pulled Deanna and me from the tank. They handed us big white bath towels. As we dried ourselves off, I saw the audience leaving. We were in some kind of outdoor theater.

Behind me, the squid bobbed in the tank. It bumped against the glass, as if trying to attack us.

A man in a black suit approached. He was tall and lanky. He had short brown hair on top of a pale, square face. He wasn't smiling. He kept his eyes on Deanna and me without blinking.

"Very good show," he said. His voice was deep and low. "Very entertaining." He glanced over our shoulders at the creature bobbing in the tank.

"The squid almost won that fight," he said, rubbing his slender chin. "We'll give him another chance — *real soon.*"

"Wh-what's going on here?" I stammered.

"Who are you?" Deanna cried. "Where are we?"

The man in the black suit didn't reply. He studied us for a long moment. His mouth twisted in disgust. "That squid was just a *little* scare," he said finally. "The *big* scares come later."

He motioned to the two clowns who had rescued us. They grabbed Deanna and me and started to drag us out of the outdoor theater.

"Where are you taking us?" I cried. "Who are you? What's going on here?"

"You can't do this!" Deanna shouted.

The tall man made a shooing motion with both hands. "Take them," he ordered the clowns.

They dragged us to a blue-and-red polka-dotted golf cart. "Get in," one of the clowns said. "Don't make trouble."

We squeezed into the cart. The clown started up the small engine, and we began to glide along a narrow street. I saw tall trees on both sides. Nothing but woods.

I poked Deanna when I spotted a green street sign on a pole: CLOWN STREET. I shivered.

The clown driving the cart suddenly spoke up. "Don't ever ask him questions," he said. "He doesn't like questions. Remember — he talks to you. You don't talk to him."

"I don't get it," I said. "Who is he?"

"Who is he?" For some reason, that made both clowns laugh. "He's The Frightener. That's who he is, kiddo. Ask him any more questions, he'll send you to the bear cage."

The bear cage?

The cart made a sharp turn into a gravel driveway. At the top of the driveway, I could see a huge house, gray and white, spread over a wide green lawn. A tall mansion with chimneys everywhere and a million windows, all dark. A tall hedge wrapped around the house as if protecting it.

"Where are you taking us?" I demanded.

"To the Clown Street Hotel," one of them said. Then they both laughed again.

It didn't take long to figure out why they were laughing. The Clown Street Hotel was actually a prison. A gray-uniformed prison guard led Deanna and me through some kind of metal detector machine, like the ones they have at airports.

Then he forced us down a long, dimly lit hall with barred cells on both sides. Sad-looking clowns sat silently on wooden benches, or talked quietly to the clowns in the neighboring cells.

Deanna and I were shoved into a small cell. "Can't we get some dry clothes?" Deanna asked the guard. "We're totally soaked."

"You'll dry out," he muttered. He locked the cell door and hurried away.

Deanna and I stared at each other. We didn't speak. I think we were both in shock. Dripping wet and exhausted, and aching from the battle with the giant squid, I just wanted to lie down. To hide somewhere and think.

But a fierce roar made me jump — and shocked me out of my weariness. Suddenly alert, I gripped the bars on the front of our cell and listened.

Another roar rang out against the prison walls.

"It's . . . a bear," Deanna whispered, huddled close beside me.

Down the row of cells, I heard a struggle. Men shouting. A few seconds later, I watched through the bars as two gray-uniformed guards dragged a white-faced clown down the hallway.

"No! Please — please —" the clown shrieked. "Not the bear cage! Not the bear cage! Noooo!"

I heard the bear roar again. So close. The sound sent chill after chill down my back.

"Please — no! Not the bear cage!" the clown begged.

But the guards dragged him away. I tried to see where they were taking him. But he was out of sight. I could still hear him pleading and begging.

Then I heard another terrifying roar.

And then applause. It sounded like a big crowd. Clapping and shouting and cheering.

Deanna and I stood there staring at each other, our hands gripping the bars. Down the row of cells, I could see other clowns standing stiffly, everyone silent, listening to the angry roars and cheering crowd.

And then a really thunderous roar, followed by a man's horrifying scream.

Cheers and wild applause by the crowd.

The clown in the cell next to us muttered, "Poor guy. He's . . . he's bear meat."

I turned to the voice. I couldn't see the man. He was covered in deep shadow. But then he moved up to the bars between our cells — and I let out a cry.

"Uncle Theo!" I shouted.

I darted over to him. He was in his Murder the Clown costume. We tried to hug each other through the bars, but it was impossible.

"I don't believe it," he kept muttering. "I don't believe it. Ray, what are you doing here? How did this happen?"

Deanna stepped up beside me. "How are you, Theo?" she asked. "Are you okay?"

"Deanna? You're here, too?" Uncle Theo cried.

"We came to rescue you," I said.

He squinted at me through the bars. "But that's impossible. The security at this prison is very tight. There's no way we can escape."

He grabbed my shoulder. "I didn't think you'd come to the circus. They forced me to Clown Street before I could warn you. I . . . I'm so sorry, Ray."

"Uncle Theo, what *is* this place?" I asked. "Why are we in this prison? What is going on here?"

"Did you meet The Frightener?" he asked. "He owns this prison. Clown Street belongs to The Frightener."

"We met him," Deanna said. "He was kind of frightening. Just because he was so mean."

"He's not *kind of* frightening," Uncle Theo said. "He's *very* frightening — and deadly. I'll tell you about him. . . ."

He lowered himself to his cell floor. Deanna and I sat down, too.

Uncle Theo sighed. "It's a strange story," he began. "Hard to believe. But here we are. So we know it's true."

He leaned back on both hands. "No one knows his real name. Everyone just knows him as The Frightener." He shook his head. "When he was little, it seems he was frightened by a carnival clown. He must have been *really* frightened, because he never got over it. From then on, all clowns terrified him.

"Even as an adult, clowns made him shriek in fright and have terrible nightmares. He became obsessed with clowns. He promised himself he would punish clowns for scaring him so badly. He decided to take his revenge on as many clowns as he could."

"Wow," I muttered. "I've heard of people being scared of clowns. But they always deal with it."

"The Frightener couldn't deal with it," Uncle Theo said. "He built Clown Street Prison. He hired ringmasters and circus owners to work for him."

Uncle Theo turned to Deanna. "Mr. HahaFace, your father, works for The Frightener. He sends clowns here to be The Frightener's prisoners."

Deanna pressed her hands against her cheeks. "I didn't know," she murmured. "I didn't know my father was so cruel, so evil."

"He isn't," Uncle Theo said. "He doesn't want to work for The Frightener. He's terrified of The Frightener, too. He doesn't want to do The Frightener's bidding. But your father has no choice. He does it to keep you safe."

"Oh, my goodness." Deanna covered her face with both hands. I think I saw tears in her eyes.

Uncle Theo leaned forward and continued his story. "The Frightener makes every clown walk through a machine when they enter the prison. It looks like one of those x-ray machines at the airport. But the machine sends out a ray that makes your clown makeup permanent." He swiped at the red makeup on his face. "It can never be removed."

"That's horrible!" I cried.

"*Everything* is horrible here," Uncle Theo said. He sighed again. "We clowns are forced to entertain The Frightener and his family and all his guests."

"Entertain them? How?" Deanna asked.

"By fighting the killer squid. Or fighting the bear. We have to fight for our lives out there while The Frightener's friends and family cheer and laugh."

I swallowed. "We all have to fight?"

Uncle Theo nodded. "And guess what? The bear and the squid usually win the battles. That's why The Frightener needs more and more clowns for his prison."

He swatted a fly on his shoulder and flicked it onto the floor. "We're like this fly," he said, his voice trembling. "Waiting for someone to squash us flat."

He snapped his fingers. "Oh. I forgot one thing. When we're not fighting for our lives in the arena, The Frightener sends us out. He sends us to entertain at kids' birthday parties. And he keeps all the money the parents pay. That's how he supports this prison. Do you believe it? We go out and earn the money so that he can keep forcing us to fight for our lives in the arena."

The three of us sat in silence. I tried to think about all my uncle had told us. But it was so crazy and so horrifying, it was impossible to get my head around it.

"Uncle Theo, there's *got* to be a way out of here," I said finally.

He shook his head. "There isn't any way," he said. "Once you're on Clown Street —"

He didn't finish his sentence. We were interrupted by a ferocious roar out in the arena. Then a man let out a high, shrill shriek of pain. The crowd burst into wild applause.

Deanna covered her face with her hands again. I sat stunned, frozen in horror, my eyes shut. Trying not to picture what had just happened out there.

When I opened my eyes, I saw a gray-uniformed prison guard unlocking our cell. He tossed in two dry clown costumes. "These are for the both of you," he said. "Put them on. The bear doesn't like to be kept waiting."

34

The guard slammed the cell door shut and checked to make sure it was locked. I handed a costume to Deanna. They were both white with big blue polka dots and blue ruffles around the collars.

I turned to Uncle Theo, who stood watching in the next cell. "Do you think we're really going to be next?" I asked.

He shook his head. "I think he was just trying to scare you."

"Well, he did a good job of it," I said.

Deanna and I started to pull on the clown suits. In a cell across from us, a tall, lanky beanpole of a clown silently practiced juggling three lemons. In the cell next to him, a woman clown with a long yellow mop wig on her head sang a song softly to herself.

"Whoa!" I let out a cry when I saw Bingo-Bongo in the next cell. I waved to him. He shook his head sadly and waved back.

"They make us stay in costume all the time," Uncle Theo said. "In case The Frightener chooses us to go entertain his guests."

I could see that Deanna was fighting back tears. "I just keep thinking about my poor father," she said. "I can't believe he has to do such evil work."

"He isn't evil," Uncle Theo told her. "He's just frightened. He sends clowns here because he has no choice."

"But — but —" Deanna sputtered.

Above our heads, a speaker crackled loudly. A voice boomed from speakers all down the prison. "Silence, clowns. Silence, everyone. The Frightener has an important announcement."

"He always uses the loudspeaker," Uncle Theo whispered. "He never talks to us in person. That's because he's still terrified of clowns."

The speakers crackled again. Then the voice of The Frightener rang out through the prison.

"Listen up, clowns. This is to inform you that my nephew Freddy is having a birthday party. We want to make his party very special, don't we? To do that, ALL of you will entertain Freddy and his friends."

He cleared his throat. Then his deep voice echoed through the cells again.

"The party will be at Freddy's house. You will entertain in his living room. I'll be there. Of course, I won't be in the same room with you. I'll be in the dining room, and I'll be listening.

"Let this be a warning to you. You'd better make my nephew and his friends laugh. You'd better give Freddy the best birthday party ever. If you don't . . ."

He paused. Then he continued in a lower, menacing voice:

"If you don't . . . you will all go into the bear cage at the same time. And the bear will have a party of his own! Hahahaha!"

He laughed hard at his own cruel joke. I covered my ears until he stopped. The sound of his laughter made my stomach tighten into a knot.

I thought about his chilling words. I thought about the birthday party. More than a dozen clowns in Freddy's living room, all being funny at once. A dozen clowns jammed into the living room . . . with The Frightener listening in the next room.

Listening and judging.

Suddenly, Uncle Theo's voice broke into my thoughts. "This means big trouble, Ray. We're in a lot of danger. Why are you smiling?"

I turned to him. "Uncle Theo," I said, "I think I have an escape plan."

35

I was eager to tell my plan to Deanna and Uncle Theo. But guards were checking all the cells. So I had to wait. I definitely didn't want to be overheard.

When the guards left, Deanna and I huddled near my uncle's cell. I told him my idea, speaking in a hushed voice through the bars.

"What if we go to the birthday party, but we don't make the kids laugh?" I started. "What if we all act as scary as we can? And instead of making Freddy and his friends laugh . . . we make them *scream*."

"I get it," Deanna said. "We terrify the kids. We get them screaming their heads off . . ."

"And The Frightener will have to come into the living room to see what all the screaming is about," I said. "And when he does, we clowns surround him. We terrify *him*."

"That's good," Uncle Theo whispered. "The

Frightener is already scared to death of us. And if he is circled by clowns, scary clowns, all trying to frighten him . . ."

"He'll freak out," I said. "He'll go into shock. We'll scare him so badly, he'll be helpless to stop us all from escaping."

"It's a crazy idea," Deanna said.

"But it could work," Uncle Theo said. "We could surround The Frightener, put him into shock, and then just make a run for it. Run for our lives. It's crazy. It's a desperate plan. But we've got to try it."

"And what's the worst thing that could happen?" I said.

Deanna frowned at me. "The bear cage for everyone?"

I swallowed. "Well . . . yes. There is the bear cage . . ."

Uncle Theo poked his hand through the bars and bumped knuckles with me. "This is good thinking, Ray. Now let's pass the word down the cells and get all the clowns practicing to be as scary as they can."

It took only a few minutes for the idea to get passed from cell to cell to all the prisoners.

"This is awesome," I whispered to Deanna. "Everyone will be ready. And we—"

I didn't finish my sentence. The loudspeakers crackled to life again.

Once again, the deep voice of The Frightener boomed through the prison.

"Attention, clowns," he said. "I've changed my mind. My nephew decided he doesn't want any clowns at his party."

I let out a groan of disappointment. I dropped to my knees on the cell floor.

Deanna balled her hands into tight fists. There was no one to punch, so she punched the air. "I don't believe it," she muttered.

A hush fell over the rows of cells. I could see how disappointed everyone was.

But then The Frightener's booming laugh blared from the loudspeakers.

"Hahahahaha. Just kidding!" he said. "Just messing with you. You know me. I like to have a little fun!"

"Oh, yeah. He's a fun guy," Uncle Theo whispered.

The Frightener continued. And what he said wasn't much fun. "The bus will take you all to my nephew's house. And . . . listen to me carefully. You'd better get BIG laughs at the party. The bear is very hungry."

The gray prison bus carried all of us clowns to The Frightener's nephew's house. The bus smelled stale and pukey, and the windows were so smeared with dirt, we could barely see out.

No one spoke as we bumped along the narrow road. I guessed everyone was thinking about the escape plan. Did it stand a tiny chance of working?

We turned onto a long, smooth driveway. I stared out through the smeared window. "The house is a mansion," I told Deanna beside me. "Check it out. Tennis courts on one side and a swimming pool on the other."

"Forget about that stuff, Ray," Uncle Theo said, leaning toward Deanna and me from the seat behind us. "We need to look for an escape route. The best way to run when we make our getaway."

The huge front lawn sloped uphill. It was covered with tall evergreen shrubs and wide-trunked old trees in full summer blossom.

I pointed out the window at the far side of the lawn. "The best thing would be to cut through that tall hedge," I said. "The hedge would hide us. We'd instantly be out of sight."

"I like it," Uncle Theo said. "Now all we have to do is get the little kids screaming and force The Frightener to come out of hiding."

"Well, we look scary enough," Deanna said.

I turned in my seat and glanced down the rows of seats at the other clowns. Everyone did their best to become scary. Some of the clowns kept extra makeup in their baggy costumes, and we all used it. Now we had huge teeth and vampire circles around our eyes, and red stains on our faces.

Bingo-Bongo wore a black cape over a black costume. He had painted a black circle over his lips to make it look as if he had a gaping hole in his face.

The clown next to him held a wrinkled green shrunken head in his lap. Behind them, a woman clown had painted her face to look like her skin was missing on half her head, and her skull was showing.

And of course, Uncle Theo was terrifying in his Murder the Clown getup, with the blazing red face and the axe buried in his head.

"Poor kids," I said to Deanna. "They're going to have the scariest day of their lives."

Deanna sighed. "Maybe it's the scariest day of *our* lives."

"Bad attitude," I said. "We can do this, Deanna. I know we can."

The bus squealed to a stop. The driver opened the door. "Okay, Bear Meat," he shouted. "Everyone off the bus!"

37

We climbed off the bus. I shielded my eyes from the bright sun. Not a cloud in the sky. A beautiful day to escape.

"Hey!" I cried out when I heard a fierce growl.

I turned and saw the bear. It was chained to a stake in the backyard. The Frightener must have brought it to show the kids.

I shuddered, watching it snap its jaws and lick its black lips. It was at least eight feet tall. *No way* any of us could survive a fight with the huge creature.

Still shivering, I followed as two prison guards led us clowns through a back hall to the living room. The first thing I saw were two enormous, sparkling chandeliers hanging from the high ceiling. Then I saw Freddy the nephew and his friends.

They were cute little kids. I guessed they were five or six years old. Freddy had curly red hair and a face full of freckles. His friends were all dressed up in party clothes. They sat on the floor facing the fireplace.

When we marched in, they were having a great time, tossing popcorn at one another. But they stopped when they saw the parade of clowns.

I glimpsed an open doorway at the back of the room. I could see a long dining room table behind it. Was The Frightener back there, as he had threatened?

Uncle Theo bumped knuckles with Deanna and me. "Let's do this thing," he whispered.

We stepped in front of the kids. Murder the Clown spoke to them first, since he was the scariest.

"What yummy kids!" he shouted. "I love kids. I love them baked and I love them roasted. I like kids extra-crispy. That's my favorite."

He grabbed a little boy's arm. "Don't be afraid," he told him. "I don't bite." Then he bit the kid's hand. "Oh, wait. Oh *yes* I *do* bite! Hahahaha."

He grabbed a little girl's hand. "Wow. You need to clip your nails," he told her. "Here. I'll do it for you."

He yanked the axe from the top of his head and held it over the girl's hand. "Hold still. Sometimes I miss." He swung the axe down hard — and missed her hand entirely.

The girl let out a squeal and jerked her hand away.

Murder swung the axe over her head. "Would you like me to trim your hair? I'll be very careful."

He gave the axe a wild swing — and buried it in another clown's belly. The clown opened his mouth in a howl of pain. And fake blood spurted from his stomach.

That was the signal for all of us clowns to start fighting. We began punching each other, knocking each other to the floor, biting and screaming and kicking, falling and groaning.

Murder swung the axe again and again. Shrieking clowns bounced off the wall and toppled over the furniture. Clowns wrestled on the floor, forcing the kids to back out of the way.

The walls echoed with screams of pain, groans, and cries of attack. Bright red fake blood splashed everywhere.

I stopped fighting and turned to study the kids.

Was it working? Did our frightening battle have them terrified into silence?

No way. They were laughing their heads off.

They thought it was a riot. They were screaming — with laughter. Jumping up and down excitedly, punching each other, cheering us on.

With a long, sad sigh, I turned to Uncle Theo. "They're loving it," I said. "They think it's hilarious. Our plan hasn't worked at all. We're doomed."

38

And then The Frightener came striding into the living room. He wore a black suit with a gray shirt and gray tie. He had a shiny pink party hat tilted on his head. His slender face was an angry red.

"What's all the racket?" he boomed. His powerful voice made the chandeliers rattle. "Why are the children screaming?"

"Let's go!" Murder cried. He waved the other clowns into action.

Before The Frightener had a chance to retreat, we surrounded him. We jammed up against him and forced him into a corner. We began laughing, cruel, evil laughter.

A clown pulled out a scissors and clipped The Frightener's gray necktie in two. Two clowns squirted water in his face. Murder the Clown stomped on The Frightener's feet again and again and menaced him with the axe.

Another clown made The Frightener's nose

honk. Bingo-Bongo grabbed The Frightener's suit jacket from behind and ripped it in half. A clown tossed The Frightener's party hat away and messed up his hair.

We made him dance. We stomped on him and punched him and pinched his cheeks. Laughing . . . laughing the whole time.

"Please — stop!" he cried. "Please!" Not in his booming voice, but in a whiny baby's voice. "Please go away. I'm so scared!" he wailed.

That made us laugh even harder. We all pressed close to him, laughing in his face.

"Please go away!" he cried in his high baby voice. "Mommy! Mommy! Make them go away. The bad clowns are *scaring* me!"

And then he broke free. He dove between us and took off. He ran toward the front, then whirled crazily around, his eyes spinning in his head. Crying for his mommy, he ran back to the dining room. We heard the kitchen door slam as he ran screaming from the house.

We all froze. No one made a sound.

And then a ferocious roar broke the silence. The sound sent a chill down my back.

And someone shouted, "The bear is loose!"

39

We ran through the dining room to the back of the house. From the kitchen window, I saw the enormous bear staggering forward, chasing The Frightener around the backyard.

The bear lurched after his prey, head raised, paws outstretched. Screaming in terror, The Frightener darted headfirst through the hedge and disappeared.

"Yesss! Yesss!"

Clowns shouted and cheered and slapped high fives and did crazy dances. "We're free! We're free!" Bingo-Bongo shouted. The little kids watched, bewildered, as a wild celebration broke out.

Uncle Theo hugged Deanna and me. "Your father will be so happy," he told Deanna. He had to shout over the cheers of the happy clowns. "Now Mr. HahaFace can go back to making people laugh. He'll never have to worry about The Frightener again."

Uncle Theo turned to me. "Your parents will be happy too, Ray. When you get home safe and sound."

In the backyard, the bear raised its head in a triumphant roar. Watching from the kitchen window, Uncle Theo smiled. "I think we'd better go out the *front*!" he said.

Mom and Dad were totally happy to see me. They greeted me in the driveway as I came walking up, carrying my suitcase. I had to beg them to stop hugging me.

"So? How did it go?" Mom asked.

"Uh . . . It was kind of exciting," I said. I didn't want to tell her *how exciting* it actually was.

Dad slapped me on the back. He took the suitcase from me. We started to the house. "Well, Ray, you certainly look ugly and frightening in that clown makeup."

"Why are you still wearing it?" Mom said. "Go right upstairs to the bathroom and wash it off. I have mac and cheese with hot dogs, your favorite lunch, waiting."

I suddenly realized that after the long bus ride, I was starving. I hurried up to the bathroom and got the water running in the sink.

I rubbed soap on a washcloth and started to scrub my face. "Hey — what's up with this?" I stared into the mirror. I scrubbed some more. And stared some more.

"Hey, Mom! Dad!" I shouted. "Hey, it won't come off! Help me! It's stuck on my skin! The makeup — what's *happening*? It . . . it won't come OFF!"

About the Author

R.L. Stine's books are read all over the world. So far, his books have sold more than 300 million copies, making him one of the most popular children's authors in history. Besides Goosebumps, R.L. Stine has written the teen series Fear Street and the funny series Rotten School, as well as the Mostly Ghostly series, The Nightmare Room series, and the two-book thriller *Dangerous Girls*. R.L. Stine lives in New York with his wife, Jane, and Minnie, his King Charles spaniel. You can learn more about him at www.RLStine.com.

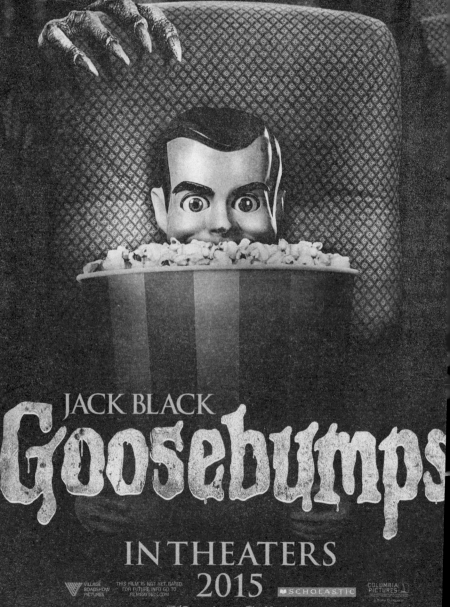

NOW A MAJOR
MOTION PICTURE

JACK BLACK
Goosebumps

IN THEATERS
2015

Catch the MOST WANTED Goosebumps® villains UNDEAD OR ALIVE!

The Original Bone-Chilling Series

Goosebumps®

—with Exclusive Author Interviews!

- NIGHT of the LIVING DUMMY — R.L. STINE
- DEEP TROUBLE — R.L. STINE
- MONSTER BLOOD — R.L. STINE
- The HAUNTED MASK — R.L. STINE
- ONE DAY at HORRORLAND — R.L. STINE
- The CURSE of the MUMMY'S TOMB — R.L. STINE
- BE CAREFUL WHAT YOU WISH FOR — R.L. STINE
- SAY CHEESE and DIE! — R.L. STINE
- The HORROR at CAMP JELLYJAM — R.L. STINE
- HOW I GOT MY SHRUNKEN HEAD — R.L. STINE